Under the Full Moon

Book 2 in the Swamp Magic Series

Bobbi Romans, author of *Swamp Magic*

CRIMSON ROMANCE
F+W Media, Inc.

This edition published by
Crimson Romance
an imprint of F+W Media, Inc.
10151 Carver Road, Suite 200
Blue Ash, Ohio 45242
www.crimsonromance.com

Copyright © 2013 by Bobbi Romans

ISBN 10: 1-4405-6901-0
ISBN 13: 978-1-4405-6901-2
eISBN 10: 1-4405-6902-9
eISBN 13: 978-1-4405-6902-9

This is a work of fiction. Names, characters, corporations, institutions, organizations, events, or locales in this novel are either the product of the author's imagination or, if real, used fictitiously. The resemblance of any character to actual persons (living or dead) is entirely coincidental.

Cover art © 123rf.com

Chapter One

Grace McKinney leaned over the dock's edge and tried to ignore the restless feeling that left her all itchy, lost in thought as she stared out into the serene Florida swamp. This was the one place where life stayed pretty simple. Survive. No second-guessing whether you said or did something wrong. Wake, eat, drink and avoid the predators. Boom—done. No drama. Well, unless you were eaten by something bigger and hungrier than you. Unlike now, where she wondered and worried about the sexy shifter, Damien. She met him while rescuing her niece from the clutches of the swamp witch Octavia. The once fabled dark entity that stalked the swamps gobbling up virile young men who caught her eye. Turns out the bad ass fable was sadly true.

Then to get slammed with the fact they killed the old hag only to have her dramatic and equally evil son rise in power. Perfect. Just fucking peachy. The bright spot had been meeting Damien. An acquaintance of Moss's. Not necessarily friends prior to the battle, the frenemies put aside any and all differences to form an alliance and really pack a punch in the fight.

She'd been so sure Damien had begun settling to life outside his secret domain. Yeah, she understood her armadillo swamp shifter friend would be nervous. Accepted it would take awhile for him to become as comfortable here in her world, which included run-ins with the public, as he'd been in his. Really thought they'd made progress. Then one evening, while sitting fireside at her cabin, Damien grew quiet—oddly so considering he'd been the one to encourage her to open up and prompted most of their conversations. Grace suspected he'd had a change of heart. When she awoke the next morning, he'd gone. She assumed back to his cave in the heart of the swamp lands. She did her best to pretend she wasn't disappointed. Hurt even.

After all they'd gone through with her niece, Beth, and Beth's fiancé, Moss, during the melee with Octavia, Grace thought she and Damien had formed a bond of sorts. Hoped Damien would chose to stay. Even considered briefly maybe they could be more than friends. The battle they'd gone through together had been grueling, and though they'd won, the war still brewed. Turned out the evil Octavia, who'd cursed both Damien and Moss into the shifters they'd become, bore an illegitimate son. Just their luck that son, Demetrius, decided to take over his deceased mother's helm in some secret and evil society.

At the very least, Grace wished Damien would have lingered long enough to say his goodbyes in person. If nothing else a letter. But there was no note. No thanks for your hospitality. Nothing.

Knew I should have offered him my bed. Least then I could have eased one thing ailing me.

When Beth took Moss back to her place, Grace offered Damien the guest room. Prude she wasn't, but that said, they didn't really know each other. She'd hoped the sparks flying between them would build, not diminish. *Guess not.*

"Knock, knock. You home?"

"Out here." She didn't want to even try explaining to her niece how she felt, because truthfully she hadn't a clue.

"I take he hasn't contacted you yet?" Beth spat.

Though they'd always been close, since the battle, they'd become ever closer. More than just family love. Her niece had grown into her best friend and confidant. She'd even let her in on the secret of her past. Her deepest heartache. That of her long missing fiancé, Henry. He'd gone into the swamps back in their youth and never returned. Until Moss and Damien explained about the rumor of the swamp, of the one shifter that chose to become one with the creature he'd been cursed with, she'd thought Henry killed by one of the many swamp predators.

"No. Damien needs time. All of this," she waved her hands around the place, "among the humans is a rather big adjustment for someone like him." In truth she was sure of that. Hiding in the swamps for years because of Octavia's curse had to have taken some sort of mental toll.

"Yeah, maybe. He's still being an asshat though." Beth leaned over and hugged her, apparently noting her goose bumped skin when she rubbed her arms.

"How long have you been out here?" Beth asked, worry lacing her words.

"Not long, but the temp is dropping quick. Want me to make us some hot tea…ah, hell. Want a shot of Scotch?"

"Now you're talking." Beth piped up.

"You know what's kinda weird? I'd have laid money on Moss suffering the first meltdown."

"Not saying anything against your Bog Man, but yeah, I rather thought the same. But seems Moss took to town life like a lizard to a heat lamp."

Beth chocked on her Scotch at the reference to Moss and his reptilian side. Happily, it came with night vision, strength and aquatic feats that would shame the best of Olympians coupled with the sexy as hell tattoos, which in fact were silken-esque scales.

"Oh well. We all have our reasons for things. He'll probably contact me one day to explain his reason for leaving." Grace hoped sooner rather than later.

"He could have at least said goodbye."

"I'm sure he will. We've all been through too much. Speaking of, you've been holding back with the all those magical abilities of yours." Ice tinked as Beth tipped her glass back and forth smiling, yet thinking.

"Honestly? Not really. Much like you coming into your own now, sometimes it takes the extreme, like a life or death situation to unleash what's been lying dormant." Grace ran a circle over her heart."Magic is purest when used towards saving another."

"Makes sense. But that whole projection thing…you should so ditch your cell phone company." Beth teased, Grace knew to try and lighten her sadness over Damien's sudden departure.

"While the savings would be great, using projection, or telepathy, is quite taxing. It's there and I can tap it during emergencies but doing so for chatty conversations with my niece would be a bit much." She jibbed.

. . .

Damien felt like death. Being sober after a weeklong drunk held a steep price. One he now paid. His head pounded and even the low lighting hurt his eyes.

You're a complete loser. You had a gorgeous, smart woman who wanted you. And what did you do? Haul ass. Nice move, bro.

He still couldn't believe how spooked he'd become. *Yeah you did, because Grace is so far out of your league a real relationship isn't even plausible, dumbass.*

Man was she sexy. Tall, fair-haired and blue-eyed. Grace had everything. Looks and brains and she'd intimidated the hell out of him. Damn, he'd taken on all kinds of bad…and yet one sultry woman had him tucking tail and booking it back home where he remained king and secure. She was so perfect and *powerful*. Too much of both for the likes of someone like him.

He chucked the empty whiskey bottle across his chamber and watched the shattering amber glass rain down in jagged shards. He ran his fingers through his shoulder-length dark hair. Damn, but if his dick didn't get hard simply thinking about her. Oh he had it bad and she held the cure to fixing that bad.

Damn shame you're too much of a pussy to go get cured.

The sound of tumbling pebbles sent him to high alert.

Someone lurked about in his cave. Considering it sat off the beaten path in the middle of the alligator-infested swamp, it wasn't some spelunker out exploring. Damien snatched his machete and blew out the candles, plunging his domain in darkness. Whoever intruded would soon regret their chosen path.

Damien crept through the tunnels, listening for any telltale signs of movement. Sure enough, far off to the right, he made out a light scuffling. Snuffing out the last candle, he laid flat against one of the cave walls crevices and waited.

Closer the intruder came, step by step until close enough for Damien to take out.

Grumphh.

Crack.

His knuckles contacted bone. Teeth clattered. Flesh struck flesh as he fought to neutralize the trespasser, who was definitely male.

"Fuck, dude, I mean you no threat. I came bearing a message."

Each had one hand around the other's throat and one fist drawn back to strike.

"Who the fuck are you?" Damien asked in a strangled garb and strained vocal chords.

"Name's Trick and I don't want to be here anymore than you want me to be. I can assure your stank ass of that."

Oomph. Damien grinned when the kid grabbed for his stomach after he tapped it. With his fist.

"Dude, what the hell?"

"That, dude, was for calling me stank ass. This however," *Whack.* "is for intruding on my personal space."

"Geez."

Damien watched the kid double over and spit blood before straightening again.

"So, what's the message and who's it from?"

"He didn't give me his name, only the message to warn you about being around some chick named Grace."

Damien bristled at the warning. There was only one person left who held any kind of power over him. Demetrius, the son of his maker, Octavia, the swamp witch. He understood the warning wasn't a threat against his person, but against Grace. Demetrius had taken a shine to her, and Damien didn't doubt he wouldn't do whatever he had to in order to obtain her. That including threatening her and all those she held dear.

And he'd tucked tail and left her alone at the cabin.

Shit.

"Okay, message received. Now get the fuck out of here." He turned, planning to grab some shit and head back to Grace's when he realized the kid lingered.

"Not waiting on a tip are you?" The kid snickered and looked like he wanted to ask something, but wasn't sure if he should.

"Oh for Christ's sake. Ask already." He didn't have time to coddle, not that he would, but he didn't want to head down the tunnel leading to his chamber until the punk was gone.

"What are you?"

"What's it to you?"

"Nothing. Curious is all."

Something about the kid intrigued him. Big, but young. Early twenties at best and appeared more than a bit lost. Still seemed uncomfortable in his new skin. Damien wondered how long the kid had been cursed. He'd bet recently. Maybe even Octavia's last curse.

"Tell you what. Why don't we agree to say neither of us are exactly who we once we were. Work for you?"

"Yeah, works."

Though Damien didn't see any immediate harm in disclosing the animal he shared within, he didn't trust anyone one hundred percent and chose to keep mum. Fact was, he didn't know the kid.

"Catch ya around."

"Uh, yeah, okay kid."

"And dude?"

"Yeah?" Damien asked briskly as his patience fled.

"Watch your back. Freak who gave me the message, well, let's just say he's off, mentally. You get me?"

"Oh I got ya kid, don't worry about me." Damien stiffened at the reminded threat and waited until the kid left his sight before packing some weapons to race to Grace.

...

Grace turned off the last light when the phone rang.

"What'd you forget?" From as far back as she remembered Beth always forgot something behind whenever she left.

"Ha, what makes you think I forgot anything?"

"Because you always do."

"Well, no. At least not that I know of at the moment. Wanted to tell you Moss offered to head into the swamp tomorrow to check on Damien."

"No. I thank you both for your concerns, but I truly think he just needs some time. Alone. Without harassment. Please." Silence meant Beth was deciding whether to argue, and Grace prayed this one time her niece would listen and let the issue drop. At least for now.

"All right, if you think that's best." Beth sighed in the background as if she didn't agree.

"I do. Men don't like to be pushed. If and when he chooses to do that again, I want to know it was his decision and not from some false sense of obligation."

"You might be right. He does seem rather bull-headed. Well, sweet dreams and I'll call you in the morning. Oh, one more thing."

"What's that?"

"He didn't by chance tell you what he was, did he?"

Grace laughed. She'd thought Beth knew, but apparently not. "Well as he didn't mention it was some kind of secret, yes. I know what animal he shares his spirit with."

"Well for the love of God, would someone tell me please?"

"Curiosity…" Beth cut off the rest of her sentence.

"Killed the cat. Yeah, yeah, I know. But Moss wouldn't tell me. Told me it wasn't his secret to tell and now I'm the only one who doesn't know."

"He's an armadillo shifter."

"He's a what?"

"An armadillo shifter."

"Oooh, that makes sense. I remember Moss saying armor up, back in the battle we had with Octavia at the cave."

"Yes, he has control of the vessels in his body and can, at will, cause the capillaries to expand and harden his skin. Makes it almost armor-like and nearly impossible to penetrate."

"That's some pretty awesome shit. He doesn't turn into a…?"

Grace laughed before explaining. "No, just takes on the qualities of as I stated. He also has exceptional night vision and scent."

"Alright. Curiosity settled now. Oh crap, gotta run."

Grace heard the husky whisper in the background. Moss wanted her off the phone and like then. She covered her mouth to keep from laughing. She wished them all the happiness in the world. They deserved it.

The cabin was stuffy and a bit humid even in her sheer shift. Opening the windows, she took in the cool evening breeze. Perfect. Except for the eerie silence.

Too quiet.

Not a screech from the owls or chirps from crickets. She lived in a more secluded section of the swamp, but even out here, the occasional barking from dogs traveled her way. Grace grabbed the bat she kept by the bedside and crept towards the living room. She rarely locked her doors, but her instincts screamed something was off. She turned the flip-bolt to the lock on the front door and headed over to secure the back patio door.

The hairs rose on the back of her neck she couldn't pinpoint the source. She scanned the dark of the cabin, any and every shadow, yet nothing was out of place.

Her imagination must be running amok.

Shaking her head, she headed for bed. Sleep. A good night's sleep would chase away the funk she was in…hopefully. If nothing else maybe she'd dream of Damien and all the things she wanted to do with him.

"Hello, Grace."

She screamed, dropping the bat.

Chapter Two

Damien emerged from the swamp, soaked to the bone, but he warmed quickly as his thoughts turned to seeing Grace again. He wanted her safe and preferably naked and beneath him. He didn't deserve someone like Grace, but she was lonely and if nothing else maybe they could offer each other some companionship. What was the new phrase he'd heard? Friends with benefits. Yeah, he'd love nothing more. She could use him all she needed until she found a more worthy mate from her side of the world.

Images of her lithe body wrapped around his drew a storm of emotions raging within. Those ripe breasts, taunt belly and hell yeah, lean legs perched on either side of his face. A feast for any man lucky enough to catch her attention.

Down, boy. We gotta get forgiveness for disappearing before we got a shot at easing anything going blue.

Damien hoped she didn't slam the door in his face. Prayed she'd listen to his explanation. What the hell was he going to say anyway? *I pussed out and ran home.* Fuck. He'd had the entire trip over to think of something, and what'd he do? *Think about fucking her.*

He rapped on the glass patio door figuring she'd be pissed about the late hour. But after Trick's warning, he wouldn't chance leaving her alone for a minute longer than necessary. When she didn't answer he cruised around front to check for her car.

Yup, her little blue Fiat sat out front.

He slid a palm over the hood and met with cool metal. She'd been home for awhile.

He took all three small steps up to the front door in one leap before knocking with a bit more bravado. No answer. Nothing. Damien raised his fist to pound until she answered. She could be pissed later after she proved all was well. He took a few deep breaths to try and find calm, when he sensed something wrong. Scented the air, picking up one vaguely familiar aroma and tried to place the odor.

Then it hit him: he'd smelled that unique scent once before. When battling Octavia.

Shit!

"Grace, if you're in there, I'm kicking down the front door. Stay back." His gut screamed she wasn't but in case, he didn't want to knock her out.

Wood splintered as the entrance crashed down.

It took only a second for his eyes to revert to his nocturnal vision and he noted nothing out of the ordinary. He'd only taken a few steps inside the doorway when he viewed a baseball bat laying ominously still in the hallway leading to her room.

"Grace?"

He silently made his way toward her bedroom, cautious as he pushed open the ajar door.

Grace lay sprawled across her bed, bathed in moonlight, her gown up around her breasts. Above her bed on the wall, the words *She's mine* written in what appeared to be blood. Fear spiked so hard he swallowed bile.

He dove for the Grace, checked her pulse and found a strong, steady beat. Relieved, he continued scanning every inch of her for any wounds. Thankful when none turned up, he shook her gently yet couldn't get a rise out of her. He caught sight of a balled up white rag on the floor. Leaning over he grabbed the wadded cloth and took a small whiff.

Chloroform.

That explained why he couldn't wake her. Damn. Nothing made sense. Why hadn't Demetrius taken her or even claimed her? He scented no mating. So why the illusion of such? Why the warning?

She stirred, moaning slightly, and rolled until her head lay his lap. His crotch grew unbearably tight, but concern overrode everything else. He'd never been knocked out with the stuff, but had read that coming out from its effects was painful to say the least.

Her phone rang, and he saw the little silver cell vibrating along her nightstand.

Beth's name scrolled across the front of the screen and he answered.

"Beth, Demetrius was here."

"Oh my God is she alright?" Beth asked, apparently recognizing his voice.

"She appears to be unharmed, but she's been rendered unconscious."

"Unconscious? Damn you, Damien, define rendered," Beth demanded with the sounds of jangling keys in the background. He suspected she was waking Moss and grabbing her keys even as they spoke.

"Chloroform."

"He didn't...um, you don't think...?"

He sensed what she was scared to ask. "No. He didn't molest her in any way, and yes I would be able to tell."

"Are you going to stay?" She paused and he heard her take a deep breath. "At least until we arrive?"

He sensed the anger behind her words and didn't blame Beth. His lack of care or concern for Grace had placed her in danger.

"Yes. I'll be here."

Grace stirred and moaned in obvious discomfort. He tried to soothe her by whispering reassurances she wasn't alone in her ear.

Beth and Moss were at least thirty minutes away and he didn't know if waking in his arms would be a good thing or bad thing. He didn't want her anymore upset than she already had been.

He needed to board up her door, but didn't want to move her. She seemed content at the moment by the way she suddenly snuggled into him and went quiet. The moaning ceasing.

Gently he moved her head from his lap and went to move a large piece of furniture up to block the doorway. The chifferobe she used as a coat closet nearly covered the entire opening. There'd be no stopping bugs or critters from getting in, but a person would make some warning noise doing so. Once Moss arrived, he would seek a hammer and some nails and get the door back up or as close as possible.

He returned and found she hadn't stirred in his short absence. He crawled back onto the soft down comforter and pulled Grace back into his arms. This time however, when he glanced down he found blue eyes peeping curiously up at him.

"What hit me?"

"Afraid it's more of *who* hit you."

He watched as she struggled to try and remember the events, but no doubt the drug caused her to be more than a little foggy. Hell, she may not remember at all.

"What do you remember?"

"Not much, but I can tell you this: my head is throbbing."

Her head wasn't the only thing throbbing. He'd noticed how damn sheer her gown was. How those pearly buds of hers poked through screaming for attention. Attention he would love nothing more than to give, if the situation weren't so critical. If she hadn't been attacked.

"Do you have anything here for pain I can get for you?"

"No, I'm clear out. Add that to my shopping list," she quipped.

"Oh shit, I do remember something. Demetrius was here, wasn't he?" She bolted up and saw the message on her wall. "Son of a bitch and I mean that literally!" Grabbing her head she thumbed her temples as if in pain.

"He didn't…well, assault you in any inappropriate ways."

"Hell, no, I can tell that. But the ass painted all over my wall." She squinted and winced, taking in the sight of the threat still dripping down her wall.

He decided against informing her that was definitely blood, not paint. The metallic coppery odor tickled his nostrils and not in a good way. When Moss and Beth arrived, he'd clean the wall before Grace had a chance to figure out the nature of the red origin.

But just his luck, before he managed to maneuver her away from discovering his erection, her hand slid from his thigh, landing slap on the painfully hard organ. Her face turned a beautiful shade of red. Oddly, she didn't move away. Instead, she turned to him with a needy look on her face. Her tongue darted out to swipe her lips and damned if that simple move didn't call to him on a whole sexual level he'd never thought about.

"Damien, I know that…"

"Grace, we're here." The frantic announcement froze them both as a slew of curses broke loose. He caught Grace's niece Beth begging Moss to hurry and please move the furniture blocking the entrance out of her way.

Their alone time was about to end and disappointment didn't cover what he felt. Neither would it cover his hard-on as he shifted uncomfortably and snatched a throw pillow to place over his crotch.

Grace shot him a questioning look.

"Beth called right as I found you. I hadn't wanted to alarm her, but she needed to be aware of the attack," he explained.

It was going to be a long night and he figured he'd best start it with a cold shower.

•••

Grace threw her arms over her chest as both Beth and Moss raced in. She'd been aware of Damien's gaze and how little her gown covered. She'd actually thought maybe they'd have their chance. Yeah the timing sucked, but damn, the last time she'd waited for an appropriate time the hardheaded and infernal man up and disappeared.

"Oh my God, are you okay? What happened, what did the asshat do, was he alone, how did you get away…"

"Whoa, hold on. One question at a time. Yes. I don't remember. I don't know and maybe because he sensed Damien coming. There, I think I answered everything."

"She doesn't remember much, most likely due to the chloroform," Damien offered before excusing himself to the guest room. Remembering the wood she felt earlier, she could only assume for a shower.

"Nothing?" Beth shook her head in apparent disbelief. "Damn, so much for getting a jive on what Demetrius's sorry ass was up to."

"He's as evil as his mother." Moss was a man of few words, but Grace knew his words rang true.

"You got that right," Grace agreed. "Now, though it feels like I've been hit over the head with a rolling pin, there's no way in hell I can possibly sleep right now. If you two could excuse me, I'll change and come join you all for a bit."

"I'll start repairing the door."

"Door?" She caught Beth's nod at Moss before the big guy ambled out of the room.

"Get dressed and I'll go put on some tea." Beth dashed into the next room before she could ask her what they meant. *What was wrong with her door?*

She tossed on a pair of gray sweats paired with a heavy black t-shirt and headed out to investigate these mysterious repairs. Passing the gaping opening where her door once stood she found no need to ask. Moss sprang up with sheets of plywood he'd gathered from her shed, leftovers from a previous hurricane threat, and went to nailing up the damaged entrance.

"No, wasn't Demetrius. Damien kicked it in when he got here and sensed his presence." Beth handed her a steaming cup of chamomile tea. Grace blew over its steaming edge before taking a sip of the calming heat.

"Thank God for Damien," whispered, more to herself than to Beth.

"Yes. Seems you were right about him." Beth grinned at her.

"How so?"

"About what he needed."

"A kick in the ass?" Moss asked joining them.

"Who needs a kick in the ass?" Damien quizzed suddenly appearing from the guest hall.

Chapter Three

As much as she loved her niece and Moss, Grace thought they'd never leave. When Damien appeared from the shower, hair wet and shirt clinging to every decadent muscle, she'd nearly sighed in satisfaction. If the visual wasn't enough to set her heart pumping, the distinct smell of male that assaulted her senses was definitely enough to set her lady bits tingling. Wild male. Grace wanted nothing more than to pounce. Instead, she forcibly endured two more cups of friggin' ladylike tea as Damien filled Moss in on what he'd sensed and how he'd found her. Damien vanished for a spell, and Grace caught sight of him outside with a pail and sponge. He'd cleaned the paint from her wall.

Finally Beth and Moss left, but promised to return in the morning to check on her and go over plans about preventing any further attacks from Demetrius or his crew. Great. Of all times she didn't want guests. Or she hoped wouldn't if her plan worked out.

"I guess I'll leave you to get some rest." Damien murmured as if he thought he was intruding on her personal space.

He stood silhouetted in the moonlight. They were finally alone. Just the two of them with all her naughty thoughts. Admiration stirred low in her belly at how his golden hued skin shimmered in the night's silvery rays. As if he'd read her thoughts his lids lowered to half-mast as a predatory glimmer sparked.

He made no move toward her. She sensed he needed her to go to him. Prove she wanted him. And she did. Halfway across the distance she remembered she wore the ugly t-shirt and sweat pants and panicked at how dowdy she must appear. But that gaze of his squelched any questions of whether he wanted her.

Grace didn't stop until their toes touched and she had to raise her head to see him.

All around them the house stood silent and dark. All except for Damien swathed in the beams from the moon. Sexy? *Oh gawd, please don't let me drool.*

"You were attacked. I…uh…"

She was the one who should feel nervous, yet here she stood, toe to toe, with her swamp shifter. A shifter who had special night eyes, and an extra heightened sense of smell. There was no hiding anything from him, especially her aroused state. Wet, ready and anxious.

Time to take the situation into her own hands since he acted like she'd break if he touched her. Took her.

Grace slid her palms, under his tee, and up his firm, slightly fuzzy chest, feeling more brazen than she had in years. When she reached his face, she forced his head down, locked eyes with him and, rising on her tiptoes, planted one on him. Thank God kissing was like riding a bicycle. Once you knew how, you never forgot. She teased his lips by tracing them with her tongue until they parted. His gaze never left hers.

An odd rumble sounded and before she even blinked, she found herself up against her wood farmhouse table. Vague awareness of things crashing to the floor flittered through her mind, but what the hell…life was short and you only lived once. She'd learned that the hard way …

Damien lifted her off the floor and laid her across the table. He stared at her like she was a banquet of gourmet goods. Grace tried to sit, wanted the infernal t-shirt off him, but one large hand pushed her back. In one swift swipe, the t-shirt cleared his head and sailed across the room. Her jogging pants and underwear were next with her panties ending up on a lamp.

The wood was cool against her ass and thighs but not for long. He grabbed her by the front of her tee and pulled until she sat upright. Unlike his hurried pace of moments before, his knuckles grazed her sides, slow and leisurely as he grabbed the hem of the tee. Higher and higher it rose until it covered her face and was blessedly removed. She needed the skin on skin contact and the sooner the better. She hadn't bothered with a bra, as the tee had been thick enough not to worry with one. *Yay for free range girls!*

Cool air hit her chest and puckered her nipples into taut buds as he tossed her top somewhere else amongst the clutter now littering her kitchen.

He stood watching her as she perched on the table, bare ass naked. It was unnerving and exciting at the same time. Instinct had her sucking her tummy in as he continued to stare while his hands shot to the closure on his pants.

Each ting from the zippers rungs sent quivers through her. *Well, hello.* Someone had gone commando and…wow.

Abs decorated his chest all the way down to the cut at his waist, that beautiful spot on a man that screamed "follow me." As if that didn't point you in the right direction, then Damien had a small line of dark hair that rode right down to his impressive cock.

Her eyes stuck on the hard lines and bulging parts. When she brought her gaze back to his face, the hungry desire she found burst shivers across her skin. His intentions were written clear on his expression, the message loud: There would be no further interruptions, no emergencies. No turning back.

Right now, there would only be here and now, him and her.

And sex. Lots of hot, needy, give it to me now sex.

His body screamed sex, muscular and powerful. And even if for only a fling, he was hers. And she was never one to look a gift horse, or armadillo, in mouth.

He stepped up to the table and grabbed her knees, bringing them up until she had no choice but to rest her heels on the table edge. She tried to scoot back, but he stopped her. Urged her back to lying on the table. So open and vulnerable. She'd started to rise up on her elbows to let him know she wasn't comfortable until one long, slow, hot swipe of his tongue had her biting hers and nestling right back down onto the weathered wooden table.

When in Rome, she thought, feeling downright giddy.

Sensations became so strong, her knees shook beneath the powerful hands holding them wide open. Grace had long since lost count of how many sighs, squeals, and moans escaped her partially closed mouth. Her bottom lip would surely be swollen from all the times she'd bit down on it to keep from begging. Damien somehow knew when she rode close to coming and would switch locations just enough to keep her teetering on the edge. Denied her a quick release.

Finally he took mercy, and two long, thick fingers entered her right as he suckled her little bundle of nerves. It was just the thing. She didn't shoot, she freaking supernovaed right off the edge. His pumping digits and strong suction had every nerve within her rippling and convulsing in perfect harmony. Never had she climaxed so hard and long. She would never, ever look at an armadillo the same way again.

She'd just gotten a grasp on her breathing when the table creaked. She eased up on her elbows and saw Damien climbing on top.

Another creak and before she could express her concerns over whether her antique furniture could hold their weight, another creak followed by the sounds of cracking wood ricocheted around the cabin.

She locked eyes with Damien just as table gave way beneath them.

"Oh crap." she squawked, but to her utter amazement, Damien maneuvered them in midair.

"How…" she began as his body took the brunt of the landing while ensuring hers was a cushioned fall.

He winked at her before planting an earth-shattering, soul-stealing kiss on her.

"Wrap your legs around me." Husky, demanding and perfect sounding.

She did as he instructed and thought the bedroom his chosen destination. But again, Damien surprised her. And hit all kinds of right buttons she hadn't even realized she owned.

He walked them toward the porch, grabbing the throw off the back of her couch as he passed, and opened her French doors. Though the night was chilly, nothing could have penetrated the heat rising from her. He sat her in the covered swing and spread the throw about the wooden planks.

Once he'd finished blanketing the area, he stood, naked under the moonlight, and held a hand out to her.

Grace looked at the beauty before her. The man who'd captured her imagination in such a short time, who was both wild and gentle just like the swamp she'd loved since a child.

The sky was clear, the stars out, the moon high and her heart full.

Never had a moment been more perfect.

Chapter Four

Grace didn't even mind the fuzzy throw was a bit itchy against her ass. Not when she was here with Damien under the soft romantic light of the full moon. A night of not being alone, of belonging, and hopefully the hottest damn sex of her life. Well, more than the hot they'd shared on the now broken table.

Damien settled over her and his expression was fierce. So full of intent and almost a wee bit of nervousness. She hadn't a clue what someone like he, so capable and self-assured, ever had to be nervous about. Strong, gorgeous, hot and sexy as hell. Smart too.

"You are the most beautiful woman I've ever laid eyes on." His voice dropped low and husky, and the timbre even more than the words made her want to preen femininely.

"Thank you." She didn't care her voice stuttered. A naked, very ready, Damien hovered above and had just called her beautiful.

His knees parted hers, and before another thought registered in her lust-addled mind, he eased in. No hurried rush as displayed earlier. Slow, like he savored each inch within her.

In no time, he set the perfect mind blowing, friction-induring pace. Strong yet confined, and Grace sensed he struggled to hold back. Saw the proof of this etched in the hard lines of his face. Her gentle giant worried for her. Wanted romantic and soft.

Hell. She'd spent far too much time alone and with only the company of things requiring batteries. Now was the time for fast and hard.

Grace wrapped her legs around his waist and hooked her ankles together, thankful her long legs afforded her such leverage.

Thrusting her pelvis caught his attention and shredded his composure.

With a roar and shake of his head, Damien's easygoing demeanor became aggressive, and she relished the change as something within herself seemed to snap. No longer content to be classic, graceful Grace, she wanted to make up for all the wicked, wanton sex she'd missed over the years.

"Rough."

"What?" Damien asked through gritted teeth.

"Let go, Damien. I'm not a freaking porcelain doll. I need you. Like now!"

He'd needed no further encouragement.

He went up on his knees for better leverage, breaking her leg lock as rough hands gripped her thighs, spreading her wide open as he pummeled in and out. Finally, the glorious sensations of his hard to her soft, the taste of heaven she'd so terribly missed. Grace grabbed hold of his forearms, to help keep herself in place. Her nails scored indents in his shoulders, and though she'd be sorry later, for now it took all she had in her to keep from clawing him any worse. He may be the one who housed an animal within, but right now she'd have sworn she did. Damien called upon the wild something that had obviously lain dormant inside her for too long. She had no qualms letting her inner vixen out to play.

"Yes…please…oh God."

Her walls stretched to the max by his sudden growth, and she realized he was as close as she to barreling over the fantastic edge of orgasm. Wouldn't have thought he could get any larger, but he did. Everything in him seemed to change. The air around him held an odd charge about it.

His mouth set, jaw rigid and eyes shut, he roared, pumping into her before leaning over suddenly and claiming her lips with a fevered urgency. The kiss was electric and her toes curled in response to the primitive sounding grunts coming from him.

Every muscle was bunched, straining, and then she followed him over the climatic threshold.

"Yes…"

His warm seed filled her, and had Beth not said something about shifters not carrying human diseases, Grace would have panicked just then. But there'd been no need for protection. Though not sexually active, she'd been on a medication to aid with a few feminine issues, and the side effect happened to be a pregnancy blocker.

His weight was a decadent treat as he dropped, spent. He still held the bulk of his weight off her, but their bodies still touched at every nook and crook, and she loved it. Wanted nothing more than to stay physically connected with him under the stars by her beloved swamp. Grace nestled into his shoulder, and the musky scent wafting from him actually caused things to stir within again.

From no sex to nympho in one night. Wow. Had to be some kind of record.

Hell with it, I've earned the right to act the sex-starved woman.

Grace felt a light rumbling and realized he'd become aware of her heated state. She fell mute when his hardened girth returned in such rapid succession.

Something to be said for a shifter's stamina, she thought, grinning as he slowly began moving within her again.

An hour later and she couldn't have moved if she tried.

Boneless, that's what he's made me, she thought, sighing in pure content.

They laid under the stars until a slight rustling alerted her that sometime during their snuggling, she'd happily drifted off.

"The night's grown from chilly to cold. I thought it best we head in," Damien tightened his arms around her.

"I am rather chilled," she agreed, shivering while trying to wake herself up a bit.

He'd taken about two steps when a rock flew past them.

"What the hell?" he snarled out into the dark.

Instinct made Grace cling to the blanket wrapped around her nude body. Damien turned and sat her on the porch swing and, still completely naked, took a protective stance before her. She should have been more concerned than she currently was over the fact someone chucked a rock at them. But watching Damien standing before her naked as the day he was born caused her mouth to go dry and befuddled her reactions.

"Who lurks like a peeping Tom? Announce yourself!" Damien demanded into the vast darkness of her property.

At the silence and lack of further activity, he whirled, scooped her up before she could utter a word, stalked inside, stopping long enough to lock the door before taking her into the bedroom.

"Stay here," he mouthed before heading to investigate, and judging by the sound of stalled hops she presumed to put on his pants.

Grace tossed on some clothes and ventured out to see what he was up to. He hadn't told her to stay put without reason. Her shifter was up to something. She knew the witch had cursed him to share a part of himself with an armadillo, but wasn't sure exactly what all that entailed. Moss was cursed with a reptilian side, which for him meant beautiful scales that resembled the most intricate of tattoos. Moss also had the ability to skim across water and see exceptionally well in the night.

After tightening the strings to her sweat pants she padded quietly out into the living room. She found Damien leaning over a small light and apparently reading something.

"What is it this time?" she asked, sensing something else had happened.

"Seems our rock carried a note." He turned and waved a paper back and forth angrily.

"And what does it say, or dare I ask?" She came to stand so close, the heat from his body offered her comfort for what she feared the note would hold.

A reminder apparently. He shook his head, clearly agitated. "You were warned and so was she." He crushed the note in his fist and slung into the night.

"Well, gee, wonder who that's from." She huffed, rolling her eyes for sarcastic emphasis when he turned to face her.

"This isn't something to scoff at," Damien warned, the worry evident in his tone.

"No, maybe not. But I'm sure as hell not running around my own home in fear of some jerk-off either." She figured she looked like a petulant child with her hip thrust out and chin held up, but she didn't care. She would not run around in fear. It simply wasn't in her.

"It's not Demetrius I fear. He, I can handle without issue." She saw the arch in his spine as he seemed to bristle at her words.

"Oh I didn't mean you couldn't." Damn male testosterone. She'd hit a nerve without meaning to. She had no doubt Damien could pulverize the little shit, but he seemed so serious about the warning. Now she'd bruised her shifter's ego. Perfect end to their otherwise beautiful evening. *Just peachy.*

"I worry about this secret Society he spoke of during the battle with his mother. Remember, he said the Society had grown weary of her dalliances with men and cursing them for her own desires."

Grace did remember. Octavia had spent years stealing and turning handsome men into shifters under her thumb. Convincing them they would no longer fit into society and that their curse would be the least of their concerns if they dare tried to leave the swamp. Her domain.

"I wonder who they are. They weren't happy with Octavia, maybe they're unhappy with Demetrius as well?"

"One could only hope. But to discount his threats and assume would be too dangerous a mistake to make. When Moss and Beth arrive in a few hours we need to research who this Society might be. I'd feel better knowing at least *who* we are up against, other than our known threat, Demetrius."

Grace understood not knowing was dangerous. But his words "in a few hours" sunk in and she took his hand and led him back the bedroom. The next day would no doubt hold much anxiety and stress. For now, she just wanted to curl up with Damien and enjoy the rest of the night.

He followed her in silence and they undressed as they walked. Neither said a word; they didn't need to. She pulled back the sheet from what she hoped would become his side of the bed. How freaking wonderful that would be. *His.* One damn rock away from perfection.

When she got her hands on that louse Demetrius, the jerk would pay for busting her happy bubble.

Chapter Five

"Oh shit, sorry."

Grace jerked awake to Beth's startled, apologetic voice and the creak of her bedroom door closing. Confused, she rolled over and threw her leg to the cool side of the bed. But instead of a chilled sheet, her thigh encountered a warm brick wall.

Damien!

She wasn't sure what to do. It had been so long since she'd invited a man in her bed, much less wakened to one still lying next to her. She froze as snippets of the night before replayed, and her cheeks burned when she went to pull her leg back and became aware of numerous sore areas. Places that hadn't been tender in a long time.

Damien shifted closer and his morning woody rubbed against her hip.

Their early morning visitors proved to be a serious downer as Damien's erection brushed her again.

"Did I hear Beth?" Even though it was his morning scratchy voice, it sent shivers through her.

"Sadly, yes." She wanted nothing more to ignore the people out ransacking her refrigerator and help Damien with what continued to prod her proactively. Damn. All it would take was to push her rear end back a bit, wiggle and …

"Mind if I borrow your shower?"

"Uh, no. Not at all." Good lord but the man caused her to become overly hormonal.

"Damien, I meant what I said before. Please make yourself at home."

His expression at her words melted her heart. So appreciative and stunned. Like he really didn't believe how much she wanted him in her life. He kissed the bridge of her nose then slid out of bed and headed for the shower in all his naked glory. A few seconds later a shocked yowl bellowed from the bathroom.

"Is the hot water not working?" Her funky acting water heater must be on the fritz again.

"I'm afraid I needed cold this morning."

"Why? Oh…uh, I understand." Cringing at what she pretty much understood to be an uncomfortable situation, she dressed and headed out to Beth, Moss, and hopefully a steaming mug of coffee. It was the least she expected at the early and ill-timed intrusion.

Ten minutes later Damien joined them, looking every bit as disgruntled as she. She bit back the laugh that threatened to spill. Moss raised an eyebrow to Damien, which she knew meant he understood and sympathized. Then Moss's turned and nodded in Beth's general direction, clearly indicating the decision to arrive so early had been of Beth's choice.

God bless her niece and her concern, but man, Grace plotted a serious girl talk with her later. If she and Damien had any kind of chance, they'd need their privacy. Deep down Grace was a little concerned about how Damien would feel when she told him about her witchcraft background and her store. No doubt the man hated any and all magic after his past with Octavia. But the differences between what Octavia performed and what was naturally within the women in Grace's family line were large and vast. Still, he knew they had some magic in their blood, but she couldn't be sure if he related to just how deep the magic ran or about her store, Whimsical Notions. Her pride and joy.

When she'd arrived during his battle with Octavia and used her magic to help he, Moss, and Beth escape, he'd seemed fine. Of course they had just met and odds were he was polite enough not to harp over the use of magic with the woman who rescued them, via her magic. Far too much happened and too quickly for her to ever bring up Whimsical Notions. Until now. *Maybe.*

Her little shop sold everything from new standard tarot cards to antique sets found at estate sales. Crystals, candles and books.

Lots and lots of books. Not just on crafts but on every topic she'd managed to get her hands on. Granted she was biased, but she loved the warm atmosphere the place set off.

She'd bought the abandoned house on Main Street shortly after Henry was legally declared dead. She'd hoped the shop would bring her some form of peace. Indeed, it had become her haven of refuge in so many wonderful ways.

"I think I'll make a trip into the swamp later," Moss blurted after draining the last drop of coffee from his mug.

"No, please. With more whack-a-doodles running amok, I don't like the idea of you in there." Beth stood, clearly agitated at the thought of her man heading back into what she considered the danger zone.

"I'll go with him. I'd like to find that kid Trick again. I've got some questions and I think he may have some answers," Damien offered.

Grace stayed quiet. Deep down she didn't want either man heading back in, not knowing who may be lying in wait. However, arguing would merely set testosterone levels raging and would be a waste of good energy. She needed to get the shop open and do some research of her own once everyone was out of her hair and she could think straight.

"Grace, what do you think? Don't you think it's too dangerous for them to go?"

Yeah she did but as much as Grace wanted to side with Beth, she couldn't. Not without pushing Damien away. He needed to be He-man. She'd recognized the trait in him from the first day they'd met.

"Yes, I think it's worrisome, but I don't think anywhere we are right now is safe. I was here at home and look what happened." Grace pointed over to the door that was nailed closed.

"Point," Beth whispered. "Fine, but you damn well better check in every hour or so. Are we clear?" she stated, turning to Moss with a definite tone and stance that signaled he'd better answer with a yes or there would be hell to pay.

Grace always got a kick out of her niece's fiery spirit.

"Reception can be spotty, but I'll agree to try. However, don't panic if you don't hear from us for a few hours," Moss reminded Beth in a patient tone.

"I can't promise I won't panic, but I won't go traipsing after you unless neither of you has checked in by tonight. Deal?"

"Deal," both men answered at once.

Grace caught something that sounded like "pussy whipped" and the sneer Moss threw toward Damien in return rather backed up her suspicion.

Yup, she needed to handle Damien with kid gloves. You could take the man out of the wild, but getting the wild out of the man in this case was impossible.

"I don't want you staying here alone. Can your aunt accompany you around today, Beth?" Damien turned from Grace to address Beth.

"Excuse me. I don't appreciate you speaking for me as if I'm not here. I assure you I've managed just fine by myself before you came along. I happen to have a full day. I need to open the shop and go over inventory." She wasn't a child and damn sure wouldn't be treated like one.

"Shop?"

Shit! She wasn't ready to explain that yet.

"Well…"

Before Grace could shoot Beth a look to shut up, the younger gal blurted out, "Oh it's her lovely spiritual shop. Grace didn't tell you about it?"

Damn, damn and double damn.

The room plunged into silence. Damien flat refused to even look in her direction, and she prayed he'd give her a chance to explain, maybe even allow her to take him on a tour of her shop. When he started out the door, calling for Moss, she knew her chance to do so, at least for today, had evaporated.

Beth kissed Moss goodbye and reminded him of his promise before apologizing. "Shit, I'm so sorry. I didn't realize you hadn't told him or he'd even consider Whimsical Notions that big a deal. Damn but I really put my foot in my mouth this time."

"It's all right. You couldn't have foreseen his reaction or my lack of telling him. I should have, but kept waiting for the right time. I'm not truthfully sure when that time would have been…so I kept procrastinating."

"He'll come around. He…he, well, sort of seems like a bit of a hard ass."

"I hope you're right. And yes, he bears some scars. But as with a lot of things in life, time has a way of healing things we never thought possible." Grace didn't elaborate, but before she'd met Damien, she'd been resigned to becoming an old spinster. Then she met Damien and he turned her emotions and resolve, ass over end. Beth left and Grace geared up to head into town and open Whimsical Notions. She'd hit the coffee house on her way and maybe that would help shake the uneasy feelings that were settling deep. Glancing over her shoulder, she saw the all-clear. She was in fact, still alone.

Why then would she swear someone was watching her?

Chapter Six

The sense of being watched increased the closer she got to Whimsical Notions. The day was sunny, the sky tranquil blue and though she didn't detect anything wrong from the outside of the shop, she felt the warning buzz in her gut. Old magic buried deep zipped to life until her fingertips tingled from the raw power.

Glancing around she noted the streets full of patrons window shopping, but considering their small town size, that only meant all of fifty people walked about. Still, a decent number of potential shoppers.

Unlocking the door, she glanced across the street to make visual contact with the cop car parked in front of Betty's Butter Biscuits. The vehicle sat vacant and she assumed the missing officer was inside Betty's to grab an early lunch or late breakfast. But if needed, the law wasn't far away.

Taking a deep breath, she entered, scanning for anything out of place.

She turned on every light in the place and found not a thing wrong.

My nerves must have got the better of me.

The warmth of the place always settled her soul within minutes of entering. The burnt orange walls coupled with the lit candles and deep purple furniture normally would cause folks to think "tacky." But here among the crushed velvet curtains and weathered leather bindings, it struck a chord of comfort. Of peace and harmony. She even had a coffee maker ready with fresh java for those wanting to curl up and check out a few books before purchasing.

A few curious people came and wandered about with wide eyes and gaping jaws. An inquisitive older woman asked for books on crystals and how they worked. Turned out the poor woman currently battled a lengthy illness and was willing to try anything, especially older herbal or spiritual remedies. Grace chatted with the sweet lady, who requested a card for future trips. Grace didn't push any false hopes but did explain that many holistic treatments, even in the worst of circumstances, had the power to ease certain symptoms.

The afternoon continued without episode, but about the time Grace grabbed for the phone to order a late lunch from Betty's, her skin crawled as the same wicked sensation of being watched intensified once more. She'd double checked the back door when she first arrived as well as every nook or cranny with potential to conceal a person. She simply found nothing to warrant the bad vibe she kept picking up.

The "nothing" in itself creeped her out more than anything else.

Her stomach rumbled in protest, so she grabbed her bag, swapped her front door sign to "Closed – Back in an Hour" and headed across the street to Betty's. *I'll call Beth and ask if she'd like to swing by and keep me company.* No, if something bad did go down, she didn't want her niece in the line of fire.

Damien.

No. Even if the man even remembered the cell phone she gave him, he'd be deep in the heart of the swamp by now and no need to alarm or change their plans for something she wasn't even sure about.

"Hi, can I take your order?"

"Uh, give me a moment please." Her mind whirred with what action would be best.

She paid for her favorite comfort food, a grilled cheese and tomato soup and grabbed a bench by the window. The best she could do right now was remain on alert herself. She had 911 on her speed dial and would keep her phone within fingers' reach. She'd be fine. What could happen? It was the middle of the day and there were plenty of people around.

...

"You seem like a rat caught in a trap. Happy to be near the cheese but not in the situation." Moss followed him into the secret entrance to his cave.

Damien stopped in his tracks."What makes you think I'm not happy being with Grace?"

"Whoa, back up. I'm not in any way saying you aren't happy with Grace. Simply making an observation you don't seem at ease or rather *comfortable* at her place."

"Sorry. I'm a bit, uh, jumpy about the subject."

"So did you leave the television on or the toilet lid up one too many times?"

Damien appreciated Moss trying to keep the topic light, but it was none of those reasons."I'm living off a woman."

"Ahh. I feel you, my friend. It's taken me some time to adjust as well. I'm used to being the provider, not the other way around."

"Grace is…well, everything. She's smart, successful and completely self-sufficient. What the hell does she need with someone like me? A freaking broke ass armadillo shifter?"

"I don't think money is even a consideration with a woman like Grace," Moss replied quietly.

"No, maybe not. But I won't have a woman taking care of me. I need to find a way to help care for her. She deserves it."

Moss nodded with a slight grunt.

"Wait…something feels off." Damien thrust his arm out to still Moss."Someone's been here. Again."

"So much for hidden escapes," Moss muttered.

"Apparently."

Damien leaned over and gave Moss the directions to the secret entrance in back. There were only two main ways in and out. With him taking the main entrance and Moss covering the rear, they'd trap whoever the hell invaded his cave and maybe get a few straight answers as to what the shit was going on. What the secret society was about, and who the asshat was who led it.

Inching his way into the opening of the cave, Damien flattened himself against the wall, hugging the shadows like a cloak of darkness. A familiar scent wafted to his nostrils, and he recognized without sight the intruder.

Trick!

If he didn't get to Moss and warn him …

"Jesus, dude. What the fuck is it with you guys attacking first?" Moss appeared before him holding the kid up by the back of his shirt.

"Found your rodent," Moss said.

"Rodent? You so did not just call me a rodent, caveman."

Before Damien managed to defuse the situation, Trick jerked, kicked and somersaulted out of Moss's grasp. The kid's long black hair swung ferociously as he maneuvered his feet to the ground, gaining solid footing.

"Rodent? Really?" Enraged, the kid moved quicker than Damien would have thought possible and flipped Moss squarely on his ass."Rodent that, asshole."

Sure he could have stepped in. But the look on the big guy's face when he careened into the earth…well, that shit was priceless.

Moss bellowed an oomph and arched his back, bringing his feet beneath him before snapping upright again on two solid feet. Trick bowed over ready for battle, and Moss for the most looked plain bewildered that some young buck had just tossed him ass over end.

"You're going to regret that, runt."

"Yeah, bring it, geezer."

Damien couldn't refrain, he roared with laughter. "Geezer. Damn but you gotta love this kid."

"You might be able to, but I think I cracked my tailbone."

"You know what they say old man…bones get brittle with age."

Trick still stood ready to take on Moss, which had Damien laughing even harder. Moss had to know the kid meant no real harm. If he didn't, Damien doubted the kid would still be standing.

"Trick meet Moss—Moss meet Trick. Now bow to your partner and do-si-do."

"Funny…real funny." Moss snickered.

"You guys ever thought of introductions before attacking?"

Damien met Moss's stare and shrugged. "Nope."

"So what brings you back to my lair, kid? Another message from Sir Asshat?"

"Name's Trick, not kid, and no." The kid bristled.

"Fine. Why are you trespassing on my turf again?"

"I figured you'd want some information I uncovered." The kid turned his chin up. He was a proud one, but Damien understood with great pride usually a great fall cometh to knock you on your ass.

"Oh what information would that be? And kid…it had better be the truth. I'd hate to make you eat dirt." Damien added, suspicious as to why the kid would volunteer anything to a virtual stranger.

"About the jerk-off who wants your lady friend."

"And why should I trust anything you tell me?"

Damien saw Moss lift an eyebrow. Knew the man wondered the same thing.

"Because right now I've got nothing to lose, but you've got everything to gain."

Damien nodded for them to follow him. He'd take the kid to his chambers. Give him a chance to sell his spiel then make up his mind what he would do with the one person who seemed to have no difficulty finding and entering his hidden domain.

• • •

Grace finished her lunch in record time. She hadn't eaten much the day before with all the chaos and…um, things that transpired with Damien. Damn but if that man didn't make her heart go pitter patter and nether area pulse with need, all while giving her a freaking migraine.

No matter how she tried, Grace knew Damien held back from her. Hadn't fully opened up with who he was deep down. She sensed hurt, confusion and a huge wall of male pride. The latter being the hardest to penetrate. Somehow she was going to have to jackhammer through that thick skull of his. Of course her plan depended on whether he was going to go postal about her shop and background. He might not even be planning to come back to her. May just send word about what he uncovered via Moss.

Her cell broke out to a song with lyrics suggesting she get jiggy with it and she laughed, knowing Beth had diddled with her ringtone again.

"Hello."

"Hey, Grace, what's been happening with you lately?"

Faith, her longtime friend and local historian of sorts was a dear buddy, but nosey. Grace suspected what was coming.

"Not much." *Liar*. Grace bit her lip, deciding whether to involve her friend. Of course if anyone could dig any black marks in the town's records, it would be Faith.

"Gurl, don't you dare lie to me. Who's the hunk you've stashed away at your cabin?"

Boom. There it was.

"Tell you what. We've been in need on a catch-up evening. How about I stop by after work and fill you in on my hunk…and I' need a bit of a favor."

"Name your favor. It's been so damn dry in my pants you'd swear it was the Sahara. I'd sell a kidney for some nice x-rated gossip."

Grace snorted into the phone. Yep, that was her buddy Faith all right.

After the brief conversation about researching any mentions of secret organizations, Grace jetted back to the shop. That was the nice thing about living a small town life. Though the library would be closed when she closed Whimsical Notions, Faith would wait for her to get off and let her through the back door.

As she flipped the door's sign around and set her purse down, the realization she wasn't alone slammed home.

She tried to snatch her purse back, grab her phone and mace, but the thing flew from her hands and sailed across the room to hit the wall. The contents splattered across the floor.

"Who's there?" Scared shitless, Grace fought to keep the tremble from her voice, as showing any signs of fear was the last thing she needed to do.

"I mean you no harm," a small voice whispered. "I apologize about your purse. It wasn't my intention to make a mess. Only to prevent you from calling for help. I promise, you won't need any. I just came to offer a warning."

"Warn me from who or what?" Grace still couldn't see this stranger. It was as if the voice came from the air around her.

"The Society members."

"I'd love to learn more about them. Why don't you show yourself and we can sit down and have a cozy little chat."

"I wish I could. But they would discover me, and in turn find you."

"What do they want with me? I don't even know them."

"You do. You just don't realize it. They think you are a threat to what they are. What they want."

"How on earth am I a threat to a Society I'm clueless about and don't give a rat's petunia over?"

"Because you do care. Plus, one of their prime members has become what they consider a liability with his infatuation over you."

"Demetrius."

"Yes. He succeeded his mother, but they are not thrilled about it. He's proven himself a weak link in their pristine armor. They worry you can destroy him and thus prove a danger to the fabric weaving them together."

"What do you have against this Society?" Grace wasn't sure who this person was or how this woman, based on the high voice, had found her. She kept her guard up but something in the voice spoke true to her. She was inclined to believe what they were saying, even if cautiously so.

"Regardless of what my lineage indicates, I believe in harmony. The Society believes in discord from which they can gain power. This must not happen. Can never happen."

"What do you mean discord?"

"Do you remember the storm that swept through? The one that flooded the bay areas and sent many homeless? Spurned many into theft and vandalism? Chaos and madness ensued afterwards."

"The hurricane two years ago?"

"Yes."

"They caused the monster storm?"

"Yes. And from the pain and anguish following in its wake, they grew strong."

"How is that even possible?"

Silence.

"Hello? Are you still there?" Grace asked.

Silence.

"Hey, you can't stop in midsentence like that. Come back here."

"They've found us. I must go and so must you. Now. Hurry!"

Shit!

Grace wasn't stupid and felt the crackle in the air alerting her to the change in magic. A powerful entity was approaching, and by the amount of energy swirling about, a dangerous one.

She ran to her spilled purse and scooped up the contents as fast as she could and fled the store. She'd no sooner put the keys in her ignition when flames erupted within her shop. Spawned by magic rather than fuel, it took only seconds before her stores windows blew out and the entire building was engulfed.

Chapter Seven

Shards of glass flew into her side window like a hailstorm before a tornado, which this resembled more by the moment. The large flames approached her car like a menacing beast stalking its prey. She turned the key over and over and the engine continued to sputter and cough. Betty from the diner came running, and all Grace could do was roll down the passenger window and scream.

"Get back! Call 911."

Betty disappeared back into the diner, thankfully oblivious to the fact this massive fire seemed contained to only Grace's shop. Flames lapped at her car and roared from the roof, yet neither shop to the sides had even the slightest smoldering.

Grace calmed her mind and focused her energy on the ignition. Willed the engine to turn over as her fingers twisted the key.

Finally after what seemed like eons, the engine vibrated to life and she hit the gas. She'd call Betty and let her know what to tell the fire department. A report of any kind would have to wait. If these people knew about her, odds were they knew of Beth, too. She needed to get to her niece pronto.

Reaching into her bag, she groped around for her phone, but the cool rectangular device had vanished. Pulling over to the shoulder she snatched the bag into her lap and tore through the contents. Damn, where the hell…Oh shit. She bet when she raced to gather her scattered things, she overlooked her phone. Crap. Well, driving to Beth's would take longer than running to the library and using Faith's phone, so Grace made a quick u-turn and headed back toward town. She'd no sooner pulled up to the ancient building when Faith came flying out screaming about her place being on fire. How the woman hadn't fallen down the concrete steps of the building Grace hadn't a clue.

"Betty called me and said your place went up in flames and you almost burned up, too! Oh my God, are you okay?"

"Yeah, I'm fine, but I need to use your phone."

"Sure honey, anything you need, but can I get you anything? Are you hurt?"

"No, I'm fine. Really I am. I must make an urgent call."

"Okay, follow me, but you need to fill me in on what the hell happened. You don't even have a kitchen in the place."

How would she explain the unexplainable? People would need to hear what happened, but hell, she wasn't even sure. Only knew magic played a large role. Grace supposed she could blame the coffee pot. Say the machine acted faulty and pray the good ole boys who volunteered with the fire department wouldn't be able to prove otherwise. As big as the fire had appeared in her rear view mirror, she doubted much would be left to check at all.

After warning Beth and getting the assurance her niece sensed no trouble and would head straight to the library, Grace tossed out her feeble story to Faith about the coffee pot and began pushing Faith whether she'd found out anything about the Society. She hated to involve her friend anymore than she already had and hoped Faith bought her second lie about needing the information for an article she was working on about the town.

Yah, Faith had pulled up information about some of the town's elders. How rumor spoke many were close to the brink of financial ruin back in the thirties during the Great Depression, but out of the blue became prosperous. Many believed they'd made some pact with the devil as no one else during the time became as well off.

"Does it mention how many had this run of good fortune?" Grace studied Faith's expression, which turned serious as she recounted what she'd uncovered.

"Not specifically. Only that over and over, select members of the town recruited their own to hold office in major areas of the town council. Of those recruited, they, too, would prosper seemingly overnight."

"But why would anyone even write that without some sort of proof? I mean, damn, I wouldn't even begin an article about anyone in the same town I lived in without some sort of hard evidence."

"That's what's so mind boggling. I dug these out of a box I discovered the other day. The articles never ran. I researched the journalist who wrote them, and the only thing I came up with was how he vanished one day out in the swamps. His articles were buried and never taken to print."

"Where did you find the box?"

"That's the weirdest part. The box jutted out from behind one of the big wall cabinets down in the older part of the archives. I've been down there before, but not often. No one asks for the really old articles anymore. But here's the thing. I would have run across the box before now. I'm telling you, it didn't previously sit where I found it.

"Maybe someone donated the articles recently?"

"I wondered the same at first, but the box was covered in inches of dust. Enough that had anyone touched the edges at all recently, the smudges would have been visible. There weren't any. From all appearances, the thing had been sitting there for years, and I know for a fact it wasn't. Those articles wanted to be found."

Grace had to agree. The timing of discovery was rather odd. Maybe the voice who warned her maneuvered the thing out into the open? Stranger things were occurring by the second.

"How old would the members be now? Eighty? Ninety?" Grace asked, running the numbers through her head. "Could any of them still be around?"

"Well, there's weirdness number two. Or are we on three now?" Faith tossed her hands in the air swirling them in circles."Whatever. Several members just seemingly fell off the planet."

"What do you mean fell off?"

"Well, records reflect them in office. All is well, then poof!—gone. Not another word about them. Or at least a few of them. Originally, thirteen are listed. Of the thirteen, all but three simply stopped being mentioned. The names of those replacing them are written in articles, but nothing else. No retirement information, death notices, nothing."

Faith reached for her coffee mug, drew it to her mouth and wrinkled her nose when her lips touched the edge. "Cold," she muttered, setting the cup down disappointed.

"Yeah I agree," she said with a slow nod. "Normally the papers do mention where the former constituent went. Whether they're retiring to Florida or running for another elected office. You're sure nothing else is mentioned? Maybe in another paper? Have you tried Googling their names?"

Faith shot her an expression that shouted "Bitch, please, of course I've already run internet searches."

Grace couldn't help but wonder how deep this society ran within their town's matrix.

"Did you cross reference the last names to anyone currently in office?"

"Actually I'd been about to when…"

"When what?" Grace didn't like Faith's sudden dazed expression.

"What's the time, Grace?"

Tugging at her sleeve, Grace cleared the front face of her watch and saw the hands read three thirty. She and Faith had been talking more than an hour now. "Three thirty. Why?"

"Well shit."

"Faith, talk to me, what's going on?"

"I left the archives room after taking some time to research before going back over the contents. I'd planned to cross reference the last names as you mentioned. Thing is, I don't remember what happened between putting the box up and two hours later getting the call from Betty about your place being on fire."

"You're missing two hours?" Grace's concern grew as did the feeling big events out of their control happened all around them. None of them good.

"Yeah. Damn, let's go make sure the box is still where I left the thing, because something is definitely up."

Grace followed Faith down the old concrete stairs to the locked archives room. Faith fished around the round key ring until she found the antique skeleton key and opened the door to a strong scent of mold and dust. Grace fought to keep from grimacing as she stepped into the room. Faith took pride in her work and Grace didn't want to hurt her feelings. But although Grace loved the aroma of old books, and, hell, old money, there was a significant difference between the smell of age and the pungent mildew odor inhabiting the room.

"No, no. Oh damn. I placed the box right here on this shelf." Faith looked bewildered and angry, though she couldn't have known what they were up against. Grace didn't even know.

"Does anyone other than you have keys? A back-up key in case you lose yours?"

"No. All the other keys were lost years ago, and the city said when and if the time came that this key," she dangled the object in front of her, "disappeared, they planned on re-keying the door with a more up-to-date lock system.

They hadn't a chance to brainstorm more before the door to the old room slammed shut. Both nearly jumped out of their skin. The room held no windows, so Grace knew nothing except that someone on the other side of the door—or *magic*—could have caused it.

"What in the world could have made that happen?" Faith asked, jerking on the door.

Grace bit her tongue but suspected no amount of yanking would open the door. Something or someone wanted them trapped in this dungeon of a room. "I can't even get the door to budge. Damn thing is stuck like it's been locked or something."

Faith removed the key from her pocket and wiggled it within the antique knob. Nothing. No click to signify the lock's chamber had opened. "I don't suppose you've got your cell on you, do you? I left mine upstairs in my desk drawer when we came down."

"No, sorry. I think mine fell out during the fire at the shop." She paused to think, and then nearly smacked her head in relief. "Don't worry, Beth should be here any minute. I'm sure she'll scout around or call someone when she finds the place empty."

"She won't find the place empty." Faith cringed.

"Is someone else here?" Grace hoped someone else inhabited the place and this door thing merely a practical joke. Though she didn't find it funny in the slightest.

"No, and because of that I locked the front doors before we came down here."

"Yes, but my car is out front. When no one comes to answer the door, she'll call the police." Grace didn't add why her niece would worry. Or the fact dark magic ran amok in their town. She didn't want to add to Faith's growing concerns.

"Do you smell something funny? Something like...oh my God, Grace, the library is on fire!" Faiths scream rattled around the old room.

Grace's blood froze. They had no way out. There were no windows or emergency exits and the library was so old, no doubt the place would go up like a tinder box. Panic flooded her while she sought her memory for a spell to counteract the fire. A few things came to mind, but as she rambled spewing them forth, nothing worked. Either she spoke them incorrectly or the magic she was up against was far stronger. Didn't matter—they were in deep shit with nary a roll of toilet paper in sight.

Faith doubled over coughing like crazy. Black smoke poured from underneath the door. She grabbed her friend around the waist and pulled her down to the floor, lower than the rising smoke, before she began searching for anything she could use to barrier the opening below the door. Finding some old newspapers, she rolled them up and began inching her way on her belly toward the door when Faith grabbed her ankle.

"Those are rare, old editions. You can't use those."

"Faith, love you like a sister, but right now do you really think I'm concerned with how rare they are? I'm more worried with saving our asses. ."

Faith shrugged but nodded her head in understanding. Grace drew close enough to wedge the papers under the door, but flames suddenly licked underneath the door, stopping her dead in her tracks.

The situation had gone from bad to worse and if Beth didn't show within the next few minutes, Grace feared tomorrow's headlines would read "Two Dead in Library Fire." She didn't want to end up in some newspaper in a new library's archives.

But that's where they were headed as the heat from the fire turned the room into an inferno. Between the smoke and flames, the air had become too thick to breathe and dots floated in her vision as thoughts of her life flashed elsewhere.

Damien.

His fierce blue expression, inky hair and a body chiseled from perfection. The animal who exuded power within such a controlled man. A walking contradiction if ever. After all the years of heartache and loneliness, and damn her luck if not around to savor the experience. She glanced back to Faith and saw the other woman had already passed out.

Oh shit.

Chapter Eight

Damien plunked the bottle of Jack down center of the table before grabbing three glasses. Kid appeared to be mid-twenties and Damien bet not a solid drinker. Good for Trick, but right now, not convinced of the kid's good intentions, he was going to liquor him up for their little chat.

Damien caught Moss's attention, subtly nodding towards the bottle and shot a quick glance at Trick. Moss reached out and snagged one of the glasses, giving him a slight nod that he got Damien's intent. Get the kid drunk.

"Fill 'er up, ole chap."

Damien obliged before filling the second glass and sliding the liquid courage over to Trick and pouring one for himself.

"Thanks." Trick tossed the glass back and downed the amber liquid in near one gulp before wiping his mouth with the back of his sleeve and expelling a large burp. "S'cuse me, mind if I have another?"

Moss burst out laughing. Apparently the kid could drink them under the table, or so he let on.

Damien poured him another. "So, what's the information you have and think we want, and what do you gain from sharing?"

For seeming so young, the kid took on a quick-like expression, drawn and weary that aged him far past his youthful looks. Damien found the sad wisdom hidden in his eyes unsettling to say the least.

"I was kidnapped around age ten. I've got fragmented memories of before and after up until a few weeks ago when I woke up with more clarity than I ever had before. I can't explain why the memories returned...only they did."

Damien decided not elaborate how Octavia's death may have played a factor in the smoke clearing. Not yet at least.

"Go on. What does any of this have to do with us?"

"The facility or club, as they call the place, appeared to be in chaos. I witnessed men running up and down the halls, and the professor..."

"Who?" Moss asked, growing a bit pale in Damien's opinion.

"I don't think he's a real professor, but that's what he told us to call him during his lectures."

Kid was quick, Damien thought with a smile. One mere eyebrow had the kid pausing to explain the "us" in his statement.

"The others like me who are, uh, different, would not be allowed back among society. That the swamp would forever be our home and we should get accustomed to the idea for easier transitioning."

"Different how?" Damien asked already knowing how Trick would answer but hoping that in his explanation, more details would come out.

"All of us are part swamp animal. Natural swamp animal. You guys are too, aren't you?"

"Yes, but continue, please. These others you keep mentioning... men, women, children?" Damien's gut dropped at the mere suggestion children would have been abused in any way.

"Just a few others I actually met, but I overheard the professor talking once about a girl stolen from them. Dude seemed pretty intent on getting her back, too. Said the B.E.A.R would pay for their interference but to use all means necessary against them to get her back."

"Any clues on who the girl or the *bear* these nuts were speaking about are?" Moss asked, leaning forward with sudden interest.

"Yeah. Apparently these are people who help keep the balance in the town."

"Balance?" Damien wasn't sure he was following the kid right.

"Our makers thrive on chaos. The guys I saw running around were babbling about some major shift in leadership. Whatever went down had everyone in a panic. I overheard shouts to get the conference room set up, and with her downfall and son's succession, heads would roll."

"Octavia's death and Demetrius's rise to power," Damien muttered while Moss nodded in agreement.

"Octavia. Name rings a bell, but only one I can remember with vivid hatred is the asshat Demetrius. He always spouted how I owed him for stealing him away from his psychotic slut of a mother." Trick grew quiet and a dark angry aura swept across his face.

"Octavia stole men for one thing, and one thing only. Let's just say, that maybe it was best, you ended up with the son instead of the mother." Damien stated almost relieved for the kid though he had a feeling being with Demetrius had been no walk in the park either.

"Don't honestly know. Can't remember even being with Octavia, but it was no picnic being with Demetrius. Dude shoveled out the shit every day. He may be some huge power in the group he's in, but if you ask me, dude's dumber than a box of rocks."

"Get back to what you were explaining about the chaos and balance theory." Moss reached out and Damien handed his inquisitive friend the bottle.

"Well, from what little I overheard, one group, our group—"

"Our group, my ass. May have changed what I am, but those fuckers didn't change who I am," Damien growled, though he understood Trick meant no offense.

"Well, the asshats who fucked with us," Trick looked at him for approval and Damien nodded, "feed on chaos like one would a freaking T-bone steak. It gives them power or some shit. The other group, the ones that stole the girl, counter fights them. For every storm or tragedy they create, this other group steps in and tries to resolve the situation."

"Resolve? Like how?" Damien asked, wondering if this second bunch wasn't just another hungry power-tripping group who didn't like a little competition.

"I'm not one hundred percent sure. All I caught was the griping about how this other group interfered all the time," Trick answered with a shrug.

A weird beeping resonated through the chambers and both he and Moss jumped like someone had goosed them both.

"Dudes, calm down. Seriously, you need to take a chill pill or some shit."

Damien went in to throttle the kid and Moss, chuckling, put out an arm to stall him. They watched as Trick whipped out a small handheld device and using his finger, slid it across the screen and tapped it here and there. Damien shot Moss a funny look, and Moss leaned over to whisper something about a smart phone. He reached in his back pocket and pulled out the little thing Grace had handed him and flipped it open. He swiped his fingers across the little screen, which lit up, but nothing changed or happened.

"That's a standard cell. Only makes calls or texts," Trick said, glancing up from his phone.

"Texts?" Damien asked.

"Baby steps, buddy, baby steps. Just remember the instructions Grace gave about dialing. We'll deal with the text stuff later," Moss instructed with a serious layer of smart ass.

"You know about this texting, too?" Damien asked, surprised at how quickly Moss seemed to be adapting to the outside world.

"Oh yeah. Wait 'til I teach you about sexting. Amazing things have been happening while we were in the swamps, my friend."

Before Damien could explore why this sexting caused his friend to grin like a big goober, Trick interrupted.

"Hey, you two need to listen to this. Shit's happening in town."

Both jolted to attention.

"Fires are breaking out all over. Some mystic shop and the library are going up in flames." Trick stated reading from the phones small screen.

"What's the shop's name?" Damien had a bad feeling.

"I...uh, hold on, give me a minute."

"Damn it, what's the name?" Damien roared.

"Uh...mystic shop Whimsical Notions, owned by a...oh damn, dude." Trick was already rising, ready to jet.

"That's Grace's shop," Damien yelled as he raced from the chambers, not caring he hadn't set his traps for unwanted visitors. He didn't give a shit about his domain. His only concern was Grace. He'd made it the mouth of the cave when Moss's bellow caught his attention.

"Try calling her."

Crap, he'd forgotten all about the gadget she'd given him was a source of contact.

Yanking it from his pocket, he jerked it open and punched the number she'd given him. No answer. After it stopped ringing, he heard her voice instructing him to leave a message. Instead, he hung up and dialed again. Still no answer.

Something was very wrong. She'd threatened that if he didn't answer she'd kick his ass.

He started to head off again when Moss stopped him.

"Let me try Beth. Maybe Grace is safe and with her."

When Moss didn't get an answer, they bolted. Damien knew deep down something terrible had happened.

If anyone harmed a hair on Grace's head ...

They wouldn't live long enough to explain their actions.

Chapter Nine

Grace came to with the ragged sensation of being drug across a floor. Her head throbbed yet her foggy thoughts still went asap to Faith.

"F…Faith," she sputtered trying to get whoever was helping her to understand her friend was in danger.

"Shhh, Faith's okay. She's being taken outside as well."

She couldn't manage any other words, but Grace recognized her niece's voice and would thank her later. For now, her lungs burned and the coughing wouldn't stop.

"Hold on just a bit more. The hunky fireman outside has oxygen waiting."

She understood Beth only wanted to lighten the moment. Keep her calm, and she loved her for that. Right now though, the only man filtrating through the haze clouding her consciousness was a particular hunky shifter man.

After taking in quite a bit of oxygen from the young fireman she could admit was nice looking, she insisted on checking Faith for herself. Her friend had taken in more smoke than she and was headed straight for the hospital. The paramedics urged Grace to go, but she had too much to alert the others about. Nothing hurt, her breathing returned to normal, so going would be a wasted trip, at least in her opinion.

"I really think you should go. Just to be safe. Please reconsider," Beth urged.

"No, no, I'm fine and there's a lot we need to discuss."

The siren of the departing ambulance interrupted their conversation.

Grace watched as the emergency vehicle raced off with her friend inside and guilt plagued her for involving Faith in her dangerous problems.

"It's all my fault she got caught up in this crap."

"She's an adult and your friend. She chose to get in involved, and she'll be fine with some rest."

"I tried to tap into my magic. Attempted getting the stuck door unlocked, but I swear something blocked my power within. Nothing sparked. Like my magic had gone dormant or something."

"A spell?" Beth asked. Grace had forgotten how new the existence of magic was for her.

"Most certainly. Dark magic is strong. And if a more experienced practitioner put a blocker up—which right now it rather seems they did—mine didn't stand a chance by itself." Grace wrung her wrists irritably. She hated being helpless like she'd been back in the library. "Any chance the guys checked in?"

"No clue. Would you believe I forgot to charge my cell last night? Of all freaking times. And don't you dare say anything. Between being your favorite niece and pulling your ass out of the fire…I think I earned a free pass on any forthcoming sarcasm."

Grace raised an eyebrow, and though she hadn't intended on giving any snark, couldn't pass up saying one thing.

"You're my only niece."

"Still counts." Beth laughed and hugged her. "Luckily the guy who works on the central heating and cooling of the building happened to be passing and had keys. He's the one who helped get Faith out and called 911 for me."

"I'm worried they've run into trouble. I'm worried Demetrius set up traps for them."

"Grace, I think he was more preoccupied setting the trap for you to be worried about them."

"Just doesn't add up." Grace insisted.

"What doesn't?"

"Why would Demetrius profess wanting me, then try to kill me?"

An explosion of voices and growls erupted and heavy footsteps stormed in their direction.

Grace never got the chance to get a visual lock on Damien before large arms enveloped her and moved her away from the others. Caged her, scented her as desperate hands explored her every curve. Her he-man shook and only spoke in grunts while he continued checking her out. He appeared frightened and out of sorts and far more wild than man.

From the corner of her eye, Grace spotted Moss, Beth, and a strange guy heading in their direction. Damien went ballistic. He looked downright feral. His eyes took on a strange opulent appearance and he hissed, hunched over, ready to lash out. His large body blocked hers in aggressive fashion, as if an enemy approached rather than their friends.

"Whoa, easy old chap," Moss urged, tossing his arms out to stop both Beth and the young man from coming any closer.

"Damien, it's okay. I'm okay." Grace stroked his arm until the muscles loosened beneath her palms. Pulled his face back to see her and no one else. Went on tip toes and brushed her lips over his in an attempt to get him to ignore everything around them. Only they remained. Her heart hammered in her chest over how emotional he became over her well being. In turn this knowledge sparked a burning need only her shifter-man could extinguish. She caught Moss motioning to the others and heard footsteps began backing away from them.

Smart man.

Damien's eyes locked with hers and his ragged, gruff pants began to ease. He was still wildly on edge, but when his lips came down on hers they were careful and sweet—yet there was no mistaking the hunger. Seeking as he tasted the proof she was alive and well. His tongue swept over hers, plundered and dominated. All the world boiled down to this. To him.

Her heart ramped up and her nipples went hard as his unique scent reached her nostrils. Damien smelled of swamp and man. Of nature and predator all rolled into one decadent tasty treasure. His body bracketed hers against the wall of the building behind them, his erection pressed against her where he leaned. The marble hard bulge made her want to do all kinds of naughty things she'd never had the courage to initiate before Damien. If not for the polite coughing in the distance, she may have forgotten they were outside and not alone. Damien probably couldn't care less about an audience. Though the kiss stopped, Damien didn't move away. His forehead rested against hers while he battled to get himself under control.

"Are you sure you're all right?" he whispered against her skin.

"Yes. Scout's honor. I'm right as rain," she promised, stroking the sides of his face trying to bring his intensity down a notch.

He seemed to be trying to breathe her in and feared letting her go.

Finally when she began to grow concerned over his erratic behavior, he stepped back, giving her space, and turned to head toward the others.

The man was a walking mystery to her. One minute running hot, the next reserved and seeming to calculate his every thought and move.

Guarded and cautious. Grace knew he'd been hurt and kept a wall around his inner most thoughts and feelings. Yeah, he showed her snippets, but she wanted him to be the one to instigate opening up. Needed to know he trusted her. Completely.

"I think we should head back to Grace's and go over what we've all found," Beth announced. "The guys uncovered quite a bit of information. How did you and Faith fair before all hell broke loose?"

"Actually she dug up some information as well. I agree, let's hit my house and I'll make everyone some tea."

Grace ignored the men's wrinkled noses and instead tuned in to the younger man with them.

"Well, they may have extremely bad manners, but I don't, so let me introduce my niece, Beth, and myself." Grace stuck out her hand as she told the new guy her name.

"Name's Trick and you're right—these two dudes seriously got to work on their people skills." The kid thumbed toward Moss and Damien, whose jaws dropped. Grace couldn't refrain the giggle if her life depended on it. She liked the new guy, and guessed he'd fit right in with their small crew.

• • •

Grace set the tea out for her and Beth, while the guys dug into her hidden Beam stash that Beth showed them. Damien still hadn't uttered a word since caging her in back of the library and now slung the shots back in true parched, Southern fashion. Something had happened with her shifter, but damned if she knew what. She supposed he'd eventually open up, but prayed he would sooner rather than later.

"So let me get this straight. There's some bad ass evil group…" Beth's eyes rolled as she began her question.

"Society," Trick interrupted.

"Excuse me," Beth corrected. "Society, who causes massive storms, most likely fires, and feeds off the chaos and destruction that ensues from it? Please tell me you're joking,"

"Sorry hon, but I'm afraid they're right. While I was at Whimsical Notions, a voice spoke to me."

"Whatcha mean, a voice?" Beth added some whiskey to her tea before shooting her a worried side eye.

"No, I haven't lost my mind yet, and pour some of that in here." Grace held her cup out. She had a feeling by the time they were done comparing notes she'd need the warmth the amber liquid gave. "A voice from thin air spoke of this society and how there is another combating them. Sadly this voice claimed the society views me as a direct threat, and I guess will be coming at me full throttle."

"Are we to believe someone who can't even show themselves?" Beth gulped the tea rather than sip.

If they weren't careful a few of them, Grace mused, would end up under the table rather than sitting at it.

"I, too, questioned her motives," Grace verified.

"She?" Damien asked, finally joining in on the conversation.

"Yeah. She, and I believe her. Something in her voice and words struck me as true."

"How so? I mean, you couldn't see her to gauge her reactions or anything. Why be so quick to judge her as truthful?"

Her niece was tenacious if nothing else. Beth had made a large transformation from trusting to overly cautious since the battle with Octavia.

"I don't expect you to believe, but I hope you'll trust in my judgment. Whoever this girl was, she might be a great ally to have in our corner. I worry an even larger battle than we fought with Octavia looms ahead. Things surrounding Octavia were merely the icing on a very large cake."

"We've gathered that as well," said Moss, his expression deadly serious.

"What did you guys uncover today?" Grace asked, pouring some more tea.

It was Trick who spoke up.

"From what I've heard, and what you've said, there are two large groups at war and we're the ones caught in the middle."

Beth nodded in agreement to the kid's conclusion.

"How much do we know about these two groups, and what do we plan to do with the information we've uncovered?" Grace began pacing about the small kitchen. So much appeared to be on the line. Far more than just battling Demetrius. Actually at this point, he'd turned out to be the least of their concerns.

"We know for sure, without doubt, one group is filled with utter asshats and the other doesn't like them."

"Group two gets my vote hands down." Moss slammed his cup down, his mind made up.

"Gotta agree with Moss. Though we know squat about the bear, my gut tells me they, if nothing else, are the lesser of two evils." Damien cracked his knuckles and nodded at Moss.

Grace was at a loss as to what Damien meant about a bear.

"We don't know. Trick overheard the society members speaking about the other group and referring to them as the bear."

Grace whipped around toward Trick wondering how missed the part that he not only knew about the society, but actually was with them. Her gaze must have been murderous because the kid quickly threw his hands up in a "whoa" like move.

"Easy there. I wasn't a guest, I promise you. I was locked up there and right before they released me into the swamp, I overheard a few things amid the chaos."

Grace maneuvered around to where she could view Damien, eye to eye, while she questioned Trick about why this so called evil society would release him. What if the kid was a rat Demetrius sent to report back to him?

"And they just let you go? No strings, no bargaining. Complete freedom. Why?" Beth glared at the kid, suspicion anchored in her stiff posture.

"Wow, she's a real ball buster, isn't she?" Trick whispered in Moss's direction grinning from ear to ear.

Grace sensed his words were not from outrage, but because he was impressed Beth had noted and questioned the obvious oddity. Grace kinda liked the kid and hoped like hell his answer rang true with her.

Damien, on the other hand, didn't seem okay with the kid's blunt response and went to snatch him up by the back of his collar until she raised a staying hand.

"Told you…dude is seriously strung tighter than grandma's hemorrhoids."

Moss barked with laughter as Beth spewed tea out her nostrils. Damien's scowl proved he wasn't a fan of Trick's humor.

"Just kidding, dude, chill already. Okay, to answer your question the only reason they granted my freedom was because they wrongly thought I'd lost my memory."

"You hadn't?" Grace drilled, still not buying Trick's story.

"Yes, for the most part I had. But in the beginning I truly had no memories other than being with them. Shortly before my release, a few fleeting memories returned. I wisely kept them to myself."

"Doesn't really explain why they let you go though." Grace understood she probably came off rabid in her questioning, but she needed to be sure.

"The only explanation I can offer is that their assumption I had no memory of my past coupled with being drilled we'd never be able to return to the world outside the swamp without being killed like a freak of nature," Trick brought his pointed finger to his throat and made a slashing sign, "made it safe to release us. Maybe they wanted to test how we would react out on our own. I don't really know."

"I've often wondered if they somehow tracked our movements. Cameras or monitoring devices in certain areas perhaps?" Moss offered while seeming to roll around Trick's comments.

Which did make a little sense. Damien and Moss had both been returned to the swamps under Octavia's watchful glare. Maybe they did have some way of monitoring their movements or at the very least were able to make sure none left certain perimeters. While there was no real way to block off the swamp, there might be magical wards that would alarm them when someone tried. Would even explain how Octavia knew Beth had entered the swamp when she met Moss.

With so much to question, Grace had no choice but to go with her instincts and Damien's on whether Trick was trustworthy. Other than his anger when Trick dissed her by calling her a ball buster—she knew Damien believed the kid. She'd felt no lies rolling from him and his aura remained clear.

For now it appeared Trick would remain a part of their group. But she'd be keeping a close eye on him in the coming days.

A cell phone went off, and strangely enough, it turned out to be Damien's, though no one but she, Moss, and Beth had his number. Considering they were all standing in the same room and none held their cell phone, it screamed shit was about to get real.

Chapter Ten

Grace noted the serious, precise movements of Damien's steps. He paced the small cabin, cell phone planted in his ear, answering in strict, short yeses and nos. She couldn't quite pick up enough of his conversation to establish what the call concerned, only the serious nature of it.

"Fine. We will meet you then. What does B.E.A.R. mean? You're fucking joking, right? Alrighty then." He snapped the phone closed with a semi laugh before facing them. "That was B.E.A.R. and they want to meet with us."

"How did they get your number? The only ones privy to the private number are right here in this room." Nerves shot, Grace questioned everything. Far too many things had happened and way too fast for a mole not to be among them. Without proof, she was staying mum.

"I'm not sure," Damien mumbled, appearing deep in thought.

"In this day and age with the computer technology we have available, anything is possible," Trick mentioned.

"True." Beth nodded in full agreement with the kid.

"So what else did they say? Who they are? What's their intentions? How do they fit into all this…anything?" Grace pushed.

"Yes, yes and no." Damien came to stand in front of them all. His long legs covering the distance in two strides and though the timing was shitty, Grace had to fight to keep her gaze on his face and not trail down the body that gave her such pleasure. "Bear turns out to be an acronym for 'Beating Evil's Ass Regularly'."

Moss bellowed with laughter, earning a thud to his stomach from Beth, who chastised him to be quiet so they could listen to Damien's recap of his mystery phone call.

"Turns out there were others who escaped the swamp witch's curse, or more aptly, the Society's, and they formed their own little group. Decided as survivors to try and stop the asshats from causing all the grief and chaos they toss out."

"I like 'em already," Beth spat.

"Where do they want us to meet them, and can we trust them?" Grace asked quietly looking only to Damien. His opinion mattered most.

"Actually, I do."

"Why?" she pushed.

"Because they gave me directions to a meeting spot, from where I assume we will be taken to their headquarters. I don't see some random group not meaning what they say, bringing us to their hideout. Do you?"

"Possibly. But I'm not seeing we have much choice if we want to learn the bigger picture."

Everyone nodded in agreement.

"When are we to meet them?" Moss questioned.

"Now."

"Potty break for me then." Beth hopped up from her seat at the table and made a quiet motion for Grace to follow.

Taking advantage of the relative privacy, Beth turned the faucet on as an added precaution and drilled Grace for her take on everything.

"More is going on than what we're aware of. I believe more people are involved and that either our group or B.E.A.R.'s has a mole within their structure." There. She'd tossed her thought on the table.

"I agree, though I'm betting the mole resides in their group. I mean I haven't spoken about this to anyone other than us and the oddities started before Trick showed up. So even though I can't say I trust him one hundred percent, it rather rules him out."

"I hope you're right."

They cleaned up and Grace got a good whiff from her shirt. She still reeked of smoke. After a quick change, she headed back out to meet the rest of the clan.

Trick lingered in the doorway with an uncertainty about him.

"You think they're aware of my presence?"

Damien studied the kid a minute before replying.

"They didn't say and I didn't ask. Point is whether you like it or not, you're in our group."

Trick perked up a bit, but then Damien finished.

"It's not about whether I trust you…it's about keeping both your friends and enemies close. No offense, kid, but until we know more, you ain't going anywhere." Damien's eyes held challenge and Grace thanked the stars when Trick wisely chose not to argue.

They piled into Beth's new Jeep Explorer, which replaced her sunken hunk of junk. Granted, her other car had been paid off, but that was neither here nor there considering Octavia had managed to submerge the thing into the swamps.

"So, are you going to tell me where we are heading?" Beth asked as she pulled out of the drive.

"Head to Dead Man's Bluff."

They all glared at Damien incredulously.

"Hey, don't look at me. That's where they said to meet. Seems someone has a rather dry sense of humor at B.E.A.R."

"Ya think?" Grace teased.

Thirty minutes later they arrived at the little cul-de-sac where local fishermen were known to put in their boats.

"Nobody's here," Beth said cupping her hands around the window to peer out into the darkening environment. "Should we get out? Maybe they are watching to see if we're armed or something."

"You three stay in the vehicle. Moss and I will check things out." Trick bristled but didn't argue.

Damien and Moss got out to stretch their long, cramped legs and began circling around the place. For the most part, Trick had remained quiet, but suddenly he announced no way was he remaining in the car with the chicks. Grace would have stopped him, but hell, the kid already appeared forlorn being left with them and until he was proven guilty of anything, she'd consider him an innocent young man full of testosterone that needed releasing.

Once the dark fully settled, the gang could see headlights heading down the bumpy road. Within moments an older style bus came into view.

Damien motioned for her and Beth to remain where they were while he, Moss and Trick met with the large burly man who exited the near ancient vehicle.

"Hey, you getting tired of being treated like the little helpless woman?" Beth asked, clearly growing impatient to find out what was going on.

"Yeah. They are rather bad about the whole female thing. Like having a vagina knocks us down the self defense steps a rung or two."

"Well, they can kiss my ass—I'm going over." Beth opened the handle and Grace joined her. She wasn't keen on taking orders, no matter how well intended, either.

As they approached the guys, the big bus driver man shot her a funny expression before turning his attention back to Damien and Moss.

"It's how we roll. Don't like, don't come. Everyone else has been introduced to the group this way. I understand your hesitations; however, it's this way or no way."

"What's going on? What way or no way?" Beth asked, going to stand next to her man.

"We either agree to ride with him blindfolded or we go back home."

"Oh hell no. No one is blindfolding me. Uh uh. No way, no how." Beth shook her head backing toward her Jeep. "Been there, done that, not going back."

Grace knew Beth referred to when Octavia had kidnapped her, but she understood B.E.A.R.'s need for caution. She wasn't crazy about the plan either. No one with any common sense would trust strangers with such strong ties to the society, namely the departed Octavia, without some major reservations.

It was time to take a risk.

"I'm in," Grace announced, stepping forward.

"Me, too," Trick declared, also walking over to the side of the bus. "But dude, seriously…you drive the short bus?"

The big guy snorted and raised his chin, humor lighting his eyes.

"Are you crazy? You're going to let some stranger blindfold you and drive you off to God only knows where?" Beth asked sounding both angry and incredulous.

"Think about it. All of us have ties, regardless of how bad they are, with Octavia and Demetrius. Would you trust us?" Grace answered trying to sound calm, even though her insides were bubbling with anxiety.

"True, but we don't know him anymore than he knows us."

Grace watched the debate roll through Beth's eyes. Her niece didn't want to go, but damn sure didn't want them going along without her either.

"Fine. Let's do this."

Moss pulled Beth protectively into the crook of his arm.

The burly guy didn't seem the least bit offended by any of their hesitations and waited patiently in the driver's seat for them to load up. After everyone took their seats—Beth with Moss, she with Damien and Trick clear in the back by the emergency door—Branch, as he claimed he was named, blindfolded them.

You didn't have to be magically inclined to feel the tension roiling off everyone. What choice did they really have? None. If there was even a shot in hell they could get some answers and end all this shit, she was taking it.

Grace just prayed the ending came with a happily ever after… and not the other kind. The dead kind.

Chapter Eleven

They hadn't even made it halfway to headquarters before shit happened. One minute they sat blindfolded on the short bus heading to meet with the ones claiming to have the answers to their questions, the next minute they were ass over end.

Grace heard the explosion at the same time as the others, and ripped her blindfold off to see the bus teeter off its wheels and slide down the highway on its side. Sparks flew as metal met asphalt in a hideous scraping motion.

Thunderous shots rang out, as shattering windows that rained glass down upon them all.

"Get to the front of the bus," Branch bellowed amid the pandemonium. "The shots are coming from behind us." The tree-sized man wobbled down the center aisle before the bus had even come to a stop. He had a gun in one hand and a radio in the other.

"B.E.A.R. to base—we've an emergency." Grace prayed the walkie worked with the ungodly reception in these parts.

"Keep behind the seats until I tell you otherwise." So much for that advice, Grace thought when both Damien and Moss jumped out an open window.

"They have guns and you don't. Get your dumbass back on this bus," Beth demanded, threatening to follow the guys if they didn't listen. *Pssshhht*

Grace breathed a sigh of relief when the radio cackled to life.

"We're almost to you now, Branch. Just tell everyone to lay low. Help's on the way. Base out."

"Ten-four, read you loud and clear, my friend."

A boom ricocheted around the bus. Branch fired back, though did so blindly since he'd already commented he couldn't actually see anyone. Yet the rounds he fired had the bus vibrating from the sheer volume.

Out of nowhere they heard a stream of curses and grunts. Grace peeked from sheltering behind a seat to see both Trick and Damien dragging two beat souls towards the bus. One man appeared far too frail to be involved in the physical fights he must have placed himself in. The other, a kid younger than even Trick, fought tooth and nail to escape the death grip Trick had on him. Answering her unspoken question of whether those were the only two behind the attack, more shots rang out. Unfortunately, none from Branch's gun. Both men being drug over to the bus collapsed in Moss's and Trick's arms.

Grace screamed for them to get their asses back on the bus. Whoever the hell was the third attacker had sharp shooter aim. Then out of the blue, the attack ended. The boondocks area they were in became deathly silent. Branch continued scanning out the back of the bus while Damien and Trick clamored back on.

Sounds of screeching brakes were music to her ears as Branch, more to himself than anyone in particular, announced, "Better late than never. Cavalry arrived."

Damien made his way to where she crouched. Grabbing her by the shoulders, he scanned her up one side and down the other.

"You are unharmed?" More of a growl than actual words.

"I'm fine. Quit worrying so much about me. I'm a woman, not a moron. I took cover. Unlike someone I know who went into a gun fight with only a wicked sense of smell," she pointed out for good measure.

"Who showed up dragging who?" His raised brow proved she wouldn't win this battle.

"'Bout damn time you 'tards finally bothered to show," Branch said gruffly to the men racing towards the bus.

"Anyone hurt?" a tall lanky man with an accent Grace couldn't quite place asked.

"No, but the bus took extensive damage. Boss man is going to have to drop some serious dough on the repairs." Branch walked around surveying the damage.

Grace cleared her throat, a hint introductions needed to be made.

The towering man walked over and extended a hand in greeting. Well, attempted to, but Damien jumped in front and near hissed at the man.

"Please excuse rude ass over there and allow me to properly introduce myself and these other lugheads. You've met Branch," he thumbed over to their driver, "and the blond Viking wannabe with the streak in his hair is Punge. I'm Coyt, and who might you be?" he asked extending his hand towards her.

"Mine, asshole. That's who she is."

"Damien!" Grace whispered, tugging back on the arm he'd tossed in front of her. "Excuse us. We've all been through a bit of a...a," she motioned her hand around to the damaged bus and shell casings scattered about the grounds, "and are a tad unsettled. I assume you are the backup Mr. Branch called? From B.E.A.R.?"

Apparently her use of Mr. with Branch sent the trio of gargantuan men into fits of laughter. Grace bit back an exasperated retort. She'd needed answers, not laughter. Her nerves were shot, she was tired and these men had seriously found and jumped on her last nerve.

She cleared her throat again. Thankfully, they all seemed to settle down and at least feign some seriousness.

"I'm sorry. It's just not often..." Coyt started.

"Ever!" the blond called Punge announced, chocking back more laughter.

"No one has *ever* referred to Branch as anything close to Mr. Our jobs are tedious, dangerous and all around shitass, so please excuse us if we take a moment to de-stress." Coyt finished.

Wow. With the way he put it, Grace felt like a heel.

"And please excuse me, too. Things haven't been the best for us either," she offered sheepishly. The last of her energy drained straight out.

"When was the last time you ate a decent meal?" How Damien picked up on her sudden tiredness she didn't know, but she was grateful for the strong body to lean against.

"I had a large lunch."

"A meal was being prepared when we left…I'm sure there will be tons of leftovers. We can talk over dinner," Coyt said, ushering them towards two separate large vehicles. With the others so quiet Grace suspected they, too, were running out of steam. Normally Beth would have already been raising hell about getting into more strange vehicles, yet her niece hadn't uttered one complaint when they'd been split up. Beth, Moss, and Trick entered a big black SUV with Punge and Branch, while she and Damien were ushered into Coyt's Isuzu Trooper.

Wasn't long before the vehicles turned off road onto what appeared to be a winding dirt road. A good thirty minutes and more butt-busting bumps and turns than she could count, they pulled up in front of a rather impressive compound. Considering they were out in the middle of Boon Fucking Egypt, the place appeared to be quite modern and Fort Knox secure.

She noted cameras blinking high up on the ten-plus foot fencing that surrounded the place. A look-out tower complete with guard and bars covering all the windows she could see, stood ominously to the far of the property.

Paranoid much?

Out of the corner of her eye, she watched Coyt press his thumb against a small black pad and a buzzing sounded before the gates slowly rolled open.

Wow. Shit like the security features they had here didn't come cheap. Someone within this organization had some serious money. Maybe like the kind she and Faith had read about. Poor people striking it suddenly rich overnight. Though all the monitoring should have settled her nerves, she experienced the opposite emotion. Unease being at the mercy of virtual strangers.

"You seeing all this?" She nudged Damien to make sure he caught the same high security points she did. His sharp nod and intent look proved he had. He squeezed her hand in a reassuring way.

"Home sweet home," Coyt announced pleasantly.

"Big home," Damien muttered.

"Well it houses some really big people. You noticed the size of Branch's neck?" Grace heard the humor, but even Damien seemed edgy judging by his challenging reply.

"Bigger they are, harder they fall."

Coyt didn't seem to take offense to Damien's statement. Instead, the man just shrugged and motioned for them to follow him through the ceiling-high massive front doors.

Beth, Moss, and Trick caught up with them at the foyer. Punge barreled past like his pants were on fire and shouted out "honey, were home" while he beelined toward the back. Grace realized his direction when the mouthwatering smell of something divine hit her nose. The loud grumbling from her stomach caught everyone in the near vicinity's attention and broke the tension into laughter.

They were ushered down a long hallway where thankfully the aromatic scent of home cooking became stronger. Grace couldn't get past the warm rustic feel of the interior. While on the outside the place more looked like a new age, steel cool fortress, the inside reminded her of some kind of mountain ski lodge. Rich wood furniture, thick wooly rugs and humongous fireplaces sat in nearly every corner. The ceilings were well past ten feet. Of course the men they followed needed every bit of the extra headspace. The whole scene had a familiar appearance.

Oh shit. The freaking Shining. The place resembled the lodge from her favorite horror movie.

Finally the hallway ended to the opening of a beautiful dining hall.

"Damn, they're all corn fed, aren't they?" Beth whispered, obviously in awe of the giants seated around the enormous wooden farm table.

Grace could only nod at the sight.

Each more occupied with digging into the numerous platters and bowls than with the newbies standing before them.

A loud belch to their right reverted attention back toward Coyt, though Branch's red face made it clear who the offender was.

"We've company among us. Why don't you take a breath from Hoovering the food and introduce yourselves," Coyt suggested, shooting death glares at Branch.

A loud clattering drew the group's gazes to the left where another lumberjack-size man grabbed plates off a large maple wood credenza and was settling to dive in for the feast.

"Yo, pretty ladies. Name's Slick, but for such lovelies you can call me anytime." A thin man stood and bowed before them. It wasn't just Damien who bristled at the man's innuendo. Grace caught Beth trying to settle Moss down from his agitated state. Didn't stop his menacing glare at the man or the possessive arm he wound around Beth's waist.

"Ignore Fido over here, I'm Red and it's a pleasure to make your acquaintance." A rather pretty redhead said, nodding her head in greeting since they were too far apart to shake hands.

"I'm Bev," a quiet woman sitting in the back said. Something about her spoke of sadness to Grace, though she wasn't sure why. The woman smiled, and for the most part appeared okay. But something in her eyes screamed sorrow.

When Branch went to stab the last steak on the platter, another of the men, nearly took his hand off for doing so.

"You freaking heathens. What's our guests going to think of us? We're supposed to be proving to them we're the good guys," Red chastised.

Grace surveyed the unruly group before them and couldn't help but wonder what they'd all gotten themselves into.

Chapter Twelve

Squire couldn't pull his gaze away from the monitor. From her. His heart thundered in his chest. His hands shook when he reached to hit zoom on the camera's monitors. After all these years of wondering. Of deep rooted desire and need to see her up close. Under his roof. Yeah he'd checked up on her. Made sure she'd been as safe as he could keep her, from long distance. Happy. But to view her so close yet so damn far tore his heart in two. Ripped open an old wound that still bore raw edges. He still loved Grace. He always would, he supposed. His first true love. The woman he'd vowed to love, cherish, and protect forever.

He'd lied.

"Figured I'd find you up here mooning away." Squire caught Bev studying him. He understood he must appear haggard and realized of everyone, Bev wouldn't buy any lie he gave. Bev, the only one who understood the link he shared with Grace. And armed with this secret, he hoped to squelch the spark he knew smoldered between them. Bev deserved more. All of someone's love. Not the ghost of a man that lingered within a dead soul.

"Scoping out the newbies." He tried to feign disinterest anyway. Maybe Bev would cut him some slack. During a few moments of weakness, he'd shared bits of his past with her. It' was wrong of him to do so knowing her feelings for him. For the life of him, he had no idea why she seemed smitten with someone like him. Bev was gorgeous. She wasn't a snob about it either. Hell, most of the time she acted like a wallflower, uncomfortable with the beauty that naturally radiated from her.

"One in particular I bet." Her voice held quiet accusation and only added to his feelings of guilt.

"So what did you pick up from them? Anything?" he wondered, trying to get her to change her course of assumptions.

"They seem okay. Curious of what they've been swept up in. I don't blame them for not trusting us. Of course if we told the whole truth…"

"No!" He whirled around in his chair. Eyes blazing no doubt, but damn if her words didn't bring the anger boiling to the surface in record time. "Bev, I mean this. Not a word of who I really am to them."

"Yeah, well I think you're being a pompous ass about the issue. If they knew the link, their trust would come much quicker. I thought this whole venture stemmed over teaming up against a common enemy. I'm starting to wonder if this was more about a chance for you to get close to her again." Bev flicked a finger towards the computer monitor frozen on a snapshot of Grace.

"I can assure you, telling them my secrets won't help our cause. End of story. I'd appreciate if you please let the matter die. "He hated being so firm with her, but she'd pushed the boundaries.

"Fine. Though I want to go on record as not agreeing with your decision. I don't think you're being fair to anyone involved over a secret this big. Shit's going to come back and bite you in the ass. Mark my words, Squire."

"Duly noted." Bev stormed out in a huff. She'd been the first he'd recruited. His only companion for many years and if things were different, he could have easily seen himself falling in love with her. Guilt plagued him he hadn't. She was a remarkable woman who deserved to be cherished. Sadly, his heart long since became cold. Died, the day he did.

He switched the monitors back on and caught the woman who held his heart being ushered to the guest quarters. His vision zeroed in on the big guy trailing in protection mode behind her.

His mannerisms around Grace screamed his familiarity with her. Thoughts of the man's hands over his Grace turned dinner sour in his stomach. Yeah, he wished her happy, but damn he did not want to see the man she found that happiness with.

He flipped the switch and turned the inside monitors off. Enough with the self loathing and pining for what could never be again.

Squire barely stomached viewing the duo walk into the same room together. Didn't trust he'd be able to refrain from ripping the guy's testicles from his body for touching his woman. He needed to get out. Needed some of the crisp night air to wipe her memories clean, *again.*

Squire slammed out the door and caught a misty eyed Bev pushing the elevator buttons. She turned her head, but he caught her expression first. He wouldn't be the only one suffering tonight. He truly was the bastard he'd been called so many times.

...

Their rooms stood across the hall and next door to one another. Moss and Beth across the massive hall, and Trick's room next door to theirs. The group agreed to meet up in an hour to discuss whether they were staying in the compound, or leaving to converge back at Grace's cabin. None of them were too sure they should trust these strangers. So far they hadn't been given a reason not to, but something felt off. A secret lurked behind these reinforced walls. Of that, Grace didn't doubt.

"Penny for your thoughts." Damien stared at her, his concern clear. He was remarkably quick at picking up her emotions and it scared her a little. The intense connection came so easily. If something seemed too good to be true…well she'd already traveled down that road once. Grace feared what may happen if things didn't work between them.

"Just wondering what they're hiding."

"Yeah, I picked up on that, too. Did you catch how none of them mentioned being the one in charge?"

"Actually I hadn't, but now that you mention that, it does seem rather odd. You'd think he or she would have made the introductions and explained more about their group. I mean, they are the ones who invited us here to team up. Right?"

"Damn straight and the fact they didn't sets off warning bells for me. The only reason for him to be absent is if he doesn't want himself—"

"Or herself," Grace interrupted.

"Themselves, known," Damien finished. "And the big question is why wouldn't they?"

"I'm not detecting anyone lying though. And if the leader is hiding for a bad reason, I would have picked up something from one of the others by now."

"Maybe, but we also can't be sure what wards or spells they may have in place."

"So you're okay with this whole magic thing?"

"I don't really have a choice, now do I?"

He had a point, but she would have felt better if he'd said yes. Would have known then he accepted the magic coursing through her veins that was an essential part of her. Not feared or worse, rejected.

"There you go again. Just when I think I've pulled you back to me, I catch the faraway look enter your eyes again." Damien came to stand in front of her. "I've only just found you and almost lost you today. I don't like seeing the distance on your face. Talk to me, Grace. Open up and tell me your concerns. Your hopes, your dreams."

With him standing so damn close the only thing to come to mind was him, her and a bed. Wall, floor, dresser, whatever, wherever—she didn't care. He rattled her when he got so close she felt the heat from his body. Images of him naked took precedence over any other notion that tried to breach the lusty haze overtaking her. And he wanted her to talk? Impossible. Question was, did she walk away or grab him and take matters into her own hands?

They had an hour to kill before meeting the others. An entire hour in this enchanting room with extra large bed.

Grace eyed the silken throw pillows and bet the sheets under the spread were silk, too. Just imagining Damien's tanned, muscled nude body against cream colored silk sheets had her insides twisting, warming, and lower areas growing wet in anticipation of the fun.

"Earlier, you offered a penny for my thoughts. Still willing to pay for what I think?" She tried to keep her face platonic enough he'd be thrown off track.

"I'd give anything to know your inner thoughts." He seemed so serious, she knew he hadn't a clue what she truly had in mind. She grabbed his large hand in both her smaller ones and pulled him toward the bed, pivoting at the last moment until his backside faced the edge. A small shove at the surprised Damien sent him sprawling over the massive mattress. The shocked look on his face empowered her next moves.

She yanked her top over her head and snapped her bra off in a speed that surprised even her. Damien made her this way. Reckless and needy. Her jeans and panties went next. When he tried to sit Grace stooped over him, which put her girls swaying right in front of his face. His tongue darted out trying to catch one of the pearled tips, but she eased back before he made contact. One-handedly she pushed him back on the bed.

My turn to be in charge and I plan to take full advantage.

Grace leaned over him, popped the button on his jeans and worked the teeth of the zipper with the upmost of caution as the material strained against his erection. Once safely undone, she slowly slid his jeans down long, dark-haired legs, nibbling here and there along large those muscular thighs and calves. He'd assisted by lifting his hips off the bed, which wordlessly told her he'd help in any way possible right now. Oh boy did he ever help. His expression screamed kid in a candy store. Or maybe teenager in a porn shop fit better. Either way the angle of his hips brought her attention front and center to the proof of his eagerness—and his anxiousness to get her mouth elsewhere.

She wanted to see that sexy chest of his, but if she got too close she knew he'd take matters into his own hands and she wasn't done with him yet. Not by a long shot. She'd earned some playtime, and damned if she wasn't going to take it.

Her hands grabbed his knees and Grace pushed them open with gentle ease. Wide enough for her body to fit between them. She tongued the inside of each massive thigh and delighted when goose bumps raced across his flesh. Apparently Mr. Take Charge decided to give her free rein and experience firsthand what her mischievous mind conjured up. When she got eye to eye, so to speak, with her prize she blew lightly across it. Watched as the engorged member jumped, begging for more than blown air. Feathered light kisses on each side, yet still refused to acknowledge what bobbed up and down for attention.

Damien groaned and reached for her even as his hips continued to pump off the bed.

She turkey necked it backwards right out of his reach.

"Nuh uh. Not yet," she whispered, aware her voice had grown husky as her own need spiked with each gentle play.

Rising a little higher on her knees, she blew more hot air across the thick, hardened length before her. Teased the muscle so that its master trembled and knees clamped closed around her as if begging her to take things to the next level.

"Remember the old phrase," he ground out, his teeth clenched, which only accented his strong square jaw line. She'd always been a sucker for a square jaw.

"And what phrase would that be, lover?" she asked, flicking her tongue lightly across the broad mushroomed head before her.

"Payback's a bitch."

"It might be, but payback has never encountered me." And she took him within the heat of her mouth. Hands wound through her hair as his hips shot off the bed. Pumping vigorously, yet refrained within the wet alcove she offered. Small pops here and there broke the silence of the room as she lost suction and regained it. Every damn thing about Damien turned her on. His moans, his voice, his honorable ways. His sculpted body so large and muscled, which, for all its strength bundled so tight, could also be so damn gentle and loving.

Damien was a living, breathing contradiction of everything she'd known.

She ran her tongue down and up over the seam lining the back of his cock, and relished in the power she currently had. Relished being in charge to tease or please the man she loved.

Wait. *Loved?* Yes. No. Maybe. Ever since the afternoon he offered her comfort out on her deck, he'd thrown her emotions into a whirlwind of torment. They'd connected during the most irrational of times and under the most irrational of events, yet there was no turning back from the strong ties that now bound them together.

But there was a fine line between love and understanding. Did she love Damien, or was it relief someone truly understood and accepted her?

The need to reconnect with him right now rode fierce. The crossroads lay before her on the silken spread. Her past and the man who'd haunted her every thought, Henry, was no more. Hadn't been in a very long time. There was only here and now. What might be with the man who struggled to allow her complete control. Deep down she laughed because there were no doubts, Damien was a man who liked to be in charge, especially in the bedroom. Or outside, or in the swamp or wherever they got enough time for loving.

"I've been patient, but must warn you…it's not my strongest virtue." His voice sounded rough and gritty and almost pained. Yup, she saw the hard lines of his jaw and sensed he held on by a mere thread.

"Scoot up some." He urgently complied with her request sliding further up the bed.

Grace crawled up his long length until she hovered just above his erection. "Don't tease. Bare…l y holding on, he rasped, eyes shut, no doubt concentrating to hold himself in check.

"No more teasing." A promise she made good on, right then.

In one smooth move, she seated herself on the jutting length of him. God, but the stretch was exquisite and she gave herself a moment to adjust. A minute later she began slowly rising, falling and fighting for control herself. Damien's hands were on her hips and the grip determined as he urged her movements.

Each breath and movement added to her heightened sensitivity. The building tension between her thighs grew enormous and her nipples swelled with need. Answering their rise, Damien leaned forward and this time she didn't duck out of reach. Instead, she arched her back, thrusting them closer. In offering and a silent plea to give attention to the tight sensitized buds.

His lips drew in one taut nipple until his cheeks hollowed from his intense pulls. Now it was her turn to ride the cusp of no return as her pace quickened. Damien, even with her atop, managed to pump his hips in timing with hers. Frenzied and impatient, they rode each other with complete abandon, not caring who might hear the commotion. She didn't care anymore about being cautious. She wanted the release only Damien could provide.

"Need…more…control," Damien rasped before in one quick move he'd flipped them so her back now lay against the silken spread and Damien hovered above her.

Her knees locked about his waist as she relinquished her control and Damien released his beast to play. Ferocious, rough and wild. He pistoned with increased tempo until the only sounds that could be heard over their gasps and groans were the twacks of flesh slapping flesh.

"Grace…mine!" Damien roared above her as he came, triggering her own release.

Later when they'd come down from the high, he reluctantly withdrew so they could shower and redress before the others arrived. She hated putting the same clothes back on, but hadn't planned on being here for more than just the anticipated meeting. Reconnecting like she did with Damien had been just what the doctor ordered after such a strenuous and testing day, but Grace still couldn't shake the bad vibe she'd carried with her. The same one she'd had at her shop.

And she was smart enough to recognize a bad omen when it slapped her in the face. Which it did a few hours later when she startled awake to being lifted out of the bed. Large rough hands had her pinned and the tacky feel across her mouth slammed home the realization she'd slept through her mouth being duct-taped. She hadn't even had a chance to kick out for Damien before a cloth came down over her face and the lights went out.

Chapter Thirteen

Damien came to awareness with a pounding head and body that ached as though someone had used it as a punching bag. Shifters, even those only magical cursed as such, didn't get sick like average humans. Though many years had passed since he'd been wholly mortal, he rather remembered the flu being about like this. His last thoughts were of agreeing to stay one more day, followed by curling around Grace. Her sweet scent lulling him into a dreamless sleep.

He forced himself to roll to his side, keeping the moan that accompanied the action as quiet as possible. He stretched his limbs, expecting to find Grace and hoping a little cuddling, or more, would take the craptastic feeling away. Only his hands ran across cool silk instead of a warm body.

"Grace?" Damien sat up and listened for sounds from the bathroom, figuring she'd gone to grab a shower.

Silence.

"Grace?" A bit louder this time hoping she had her head wrapped in a towel that muffled his calls.

Panic punched him harder than the urgent waves of nausea as he sprang from the bed to the bathroom. The white stone room was immaculate. Not a drop of water in the shower or moisture in the sink. No one had used the bathroom since he and Grace had the evening before.

He checked the chair where she'd folded and left her clothes on. Fear rooted deep when he found them still sitting as neat and tidy as when Grace originally laid them down. While she may have gone to speak with Beth, she wouldn't do so wearing only his t-shirt and not a stitch else.

He tossed on his pants, not bothering to button them and raced barefooted across the hall to Moss and Beth's room, banging on their door like a madman on speed.

Moss opened the door with such brute force, Damien jerked away, stunned the thing hadn't ripped off its hinges.

"Is Grace here?"

"No, I thought she stayed with you." Moss spoke in a hushed tone no doubt trying to save Beth from undue panic. He stepped out into the hall with him, closing the door lightly behind him. "Why don't you ask Trick if he's seen her?"

"Why the fuck would she be with Trick?" He scrubbed his hand over his face and did his best to reel back the urge to knock Moss's head off his shoulders over such an asinine suggestion.

"Whoa, settle down. I didn't mean anything like that. Only thinking she had a question, or maybe he came and knocked with his own concern while you slept."

"I wouldn't sleep through someone knocking on our door." He felt compelled to state the fact to protect his honor, but Moss far well understood this already. The man, his friend, seemed intent on trying to keep him calm until Grace turned up. No meltdowns in front of their new friends, especially if they had something to do with her disappearance. Using only his eyes, Moss motioned toward the corner of the ceiling. Without looking at where Moss directed his gaze, Damien pretended to stoop for something off the floor. Tilting his head only a fraction, he used his peripheral vision to detect the sensor.

Someone monitored the halls.

Question he wanted answered was why? He understood the need for security cameras outside the compound, but in the actual living quarters? Either their hosts didn't trust them or they weren't considered guests. Either way the monitors discovery disconcerted him.

"Well, why don't we ask Trick just to make sure she's not with him?" Moss headed across the hall to Trick's door, rapping quietly. The second Trick answered, both men silently alerted him to the monitor.

Trick stood back and allowed them entry while Moss scouted around the suite for the bathroom. Once inside, he turned on the shower and sink and motioned for the guys to join him.

"While I don't think our hosts are monitoring the bathrooms visually, I'm not prepared to take a chance with the audio possibilities. Let's speak quietly, in case it's bugged."

Both he and Trick agreed wholeheartedly with Moss's instincts. "Did Grace pop in by chance?" Damien whispered urgently, yet low as possible.

"No. I thought she stayed with you. Hell, sure as shit sounded like you roomed together with all the racket. Man, shit about came off the walls and all."

Yeah, he and Grace had gotten rather wild, but not so crazed things should have flown off the walls.

"What do you mean?"

"Uh dude…headboard, wall. Boink, boink. I really gotta explain anymore?" Trick's cocky attitude this early coupled with Grace's vanishing act left him wanting to thump the kid. Hard. Square between the eyes.

Apparently picking up the physical aggression from Damien, Moss jumped in.

"Grace is gone. We wanted to check if you'd seen or spoken to her."

"No. Actually tried to zone out the ruckus they caused last night." Even Trick had a concerned serious look crossing his face.

"Thing is, we, uh, didn't get overly rambunctious. Maybe loud, but not wall thumping crazy." Damien didn't plan on going into the explanation their position in bed would have not moved the massive and heavy solid teak wood headboard. He and Grace had *not* made the commotion Trick described.

"You remember what time all the wall banging began?" Moss asked.

"I didn't exactly look at the clock, but probably around two A.M. Please tell me you two got your jiggity on then." Apprehension crept across Trick's face.

"No. The ruckus didn't stem from us. Let me rephrase. Least not from a conscious us."

"Damn, dude. I woulda busted a bad guy's ass. I thought you two were getting it on like rabbits again. Fuck. I coulda done something." Trick slammed his fist into the bathroom wall next to him cursing up a storm.

"Sssh. Remember. We don't understand how our hosts fit into all this, and until we do, the least they know the better." Moss urged caution and quiet.

"Yeah, but man. I fucked up like royally good." It didn't take a rocket scientist to see the guilt that weighed heavy on Trick's mind.

"Look, kid, this isn't your fault. No way could you have suspected what was really going down. What I need to figure out is why I didn't awaken through the melee right beside my head. How I slept through that much chaos." Damien raked a hand through his hair."

"Slept through what, and why are you guys all huddled in the bathroom whispering? Hey, where is Grace? She head down to breakfast already?"

All three men, no matter how mighty, jumped like firecrackers went off in their asses.

Damien hadn't formulated yet how to explain to Grace's niece her aunt's sudden disappearance. It would have been wasted energy anyhow, as Trick blurted out an apology, which sent Beth into a full on tizzy.

"Where the fuck were you at? She slept right next to you. How could you not notice her getting kidnapped?" Damien ignored the sharp jabbing finger in his chest. She only asked the very thing he couldn't figure out himself. He didn't blame her for the accusations contained in her questions.

"Wait. You said breakfast. Did someone knock and announce it was meal time or what?" Moss asked, finally catching onto what she'd said upon arriving.

"Yeah. Coyt came up to tell us. He didn't linger, just knocked, announced grub was ready, and asked if I would let you guys know. Told him yeah and he left. Why?" Hope brightened her pale worried face.

"Is there any way Grace just headed down before us?" Moss quizzed.

"Not unless she went half naked," Damien reminded them.

"Well I'm heading down and asking anyway." Beth started out the door, but Moss grabbed her and stopped her.

"How can we be sure they're not involved?"

"We can't. But they have cameras, right? I'm willing to bet they aren't behind her disappearance and those cameras can show what the hell went down last night. There isn't time to pussy foot around all this."

Moss nodded in agreement and Damien knew that again, the group had been forced into no choice but to trust the B.E.A.R. organization. While he wasn't one to trust easily, he also wasn't a moron. Right now whether he liked it or not, the B.E.A.R. group was their best chance at discovering what happened to Grace.

They headed to catch up with Beth, who'd stormed out before they'd all agreed. Moss had his hands full with his woman. Headstrong didn't quite cover Beth adequately, but it happened to be the only polite term to come to mind.

Her heavy steps down the stairs echoed her level of agitation. Worry prompted each one.

"So we need access to your security tapes, like right now," she blurted entering the dining room.

The clanging spoons and forks in dishes that steam rose from in the dining hall abruptly stopped.

"Well good morning to you as well," Coyt stated, rising to walk to them.

"Actually it's not. Grace disappeared and we've reason to believe she was abducted from your so-called 'secure environment.' I mean that was one of the reasons you urged us all to stay last night, wasn't it? That your compound stood more secure than Grace's cabin? Well, so much for that theory. Now, the tapes please."

A pin drop would have caused more noise than the sudden breathless state overtaking the room by the time Beth finished blasting their faulty secure systems.

"Of course. Follow me." Coyt, too, had grown silent and serious. The entire room eyeballed one another before jumping into action with exclamations to checkout every security feature and alarm system the place housed.

Coyt ushered the group towards an elevator, slid a key card through a special security mechanism, then when a small box slid out of the wall, placed his thumb securely in its center. Within a moment, a small beep occurred and the small box maneuvered back into its hidden spot as the elevator doors slid open with a whoosh.

"If anything has happened to her after all your assurances of safety…" Damien didn't finish his sentence. He didn't trust himself to think of the possibilities in such close quarters. So far he'd managed to hold his anxiety in place. But as the minutes without Grace went on, the edgier and less grounded he became.

"Don't worry, shifter. We'll get your woman back…if, that is, she was taken."

In a flash before any thought registered, Damien had Coyt by his throat and up against the elevator wall. Red marred his vision as he squeezed. Oblivious to the others' cries to let the man go, he wanted to maim, hurt, kill. Would accept nothing short of.

How dare he insinuate Grace would be anywhere except here with him. She wouldn't have just up and gone, and this asshat dared mention her as if she'd skipped out. As if she were a mole or some other complete bullshit. It would be the last damn thing he thought or said about her. *Ever.*

"Please, please let Uncle Coyt go. He didn't mean anything by what he said."

Somehow through the fog of pure rage, the sweet, pleading voice reached him. As Damien's vision cleared, he saw the man he held by the throat. Red faced and lacking oxygen and quite near ready to die. Damien released him and backed against the far wall. Took deep breaths to try and contain the need to rip him to shreds. Beth stood next to him. Speaking in soothing tones. He didn't comprehend what she said, only that it was calm and reassuring. Trick stood between him and Coyt, trying to, he assumed, block his view of the bastard. Moss picked the near unconscious ass and with the young girl's help, assisted him off the lift.

Finally Damien sensed he could move without the need to physically harm anyone. He shook his head a few more times and with breathing back in check, turned ready to face the consequences of his actions. No, he didn't give a shit about Coyt, but frightening the girl as he had? The fear he'd seen in her eyes. Well that was different. Made him feel like a total douche.

Wisely they'd taken Coyt somewhere else, but now a man stood before them and he didn't seem too happy with the events. Like Damien gave a flying shit.

"I trust you're in better control of yourself now?"

"I'd have no control issues if you had proper charge over your compound or yellow-bellied men who want to blame an innocent woman for being abducted," Damien sneered, once again fighting to contain the anger.

"Whoa, let's say we all start over. Shall we?"

Moss appeared from around a corner and headed straight toward them. Obviously his friend was concerned over a repeat performance.

"And you are?" Beth asked, peeved and highly agitated herself.

"They call me Squire, and I run B.E.A.R. How can I help you?"

"Good. The dude in charge. Now, where are the tape recordings from last night?"

"To which tapes are you referring?" Damien sensed the man, for whatever reason, attempted to stall them.

"Look, asswipe, my aunt has been abducted and we need to review your security tapes now. Not in a minute, right damn now." Beth seethed, stomping towards Squire aggressively enough Moss shadowed her steps in case the need for obvious intervention occurred. Damien didn't doubt if this Squire man didn't take them to the surveillance room asap, Moss wouldn't be pulling just one person off a B.E.A.R. member, but two.

"Grace is missing? How? When?" Squire grew serious in the blink of an eye.

No one else caught it, but he did. They'd never told him her name. But it was far more than that. The way Squire said Grace's name, like she was a Goddess and he but her servant unworthy of speaking her name, made Damien's gut roil. Both he and Grace suspected more was going on than met the eye. They'd been right. His only concern now though was the tapes and getting Grace back. Then he'd dig into just how familiar Squire was with Grace. Oh yeah. Dude seriously would get a face alteration. Grace was his. Period.

"Sometime during the night," Damien spat, biting back the rest of his words, still reeling over the fact he'd not awakened during her abduction. And still suffering a pounding ass headache.

"Who was first to knock on her door and notice her gone?"

Hell fucking yeah. His shot at Squire came earlier than he hoped.

"I awoke to find the bed empty early this morning." Words and steel combined as Damien verbally laid claim to his woman.

Squire's gaze took him in. Shock, anger then control slipped back into his expression. The man might know Grace, but for now was keeping the information to himself.

"And nothing was out of place?" The man might be quiet, but Damien never failed to recognize a fellow shifter. In fact everyone he'd run across here at the compound was. Difference was, his animal reared as it sensed Squires was a challenger. An alpha encroaching on his turf. Their animal counterparts were rearing to get out. Prove dominance.

Yeah buddy. After only a second of recovery, Squire's holier than thou mask had returned.

"No. Nothing out of place and no oddities. Not a damn thing except waking to the flu. Not only is your compound not secure, it's apparently host to a plague of viruses as well."

"Wait, I thought Moss said shifters don't get sick?" Beth picked up on the oddity.

"Not usually. But I awoke off-kilter and would swear my head is ready to explode."

Damien couldn't miss the worried look Beth shot Moss.

"Please, Squire, we need to review those tapes immediately. My aunt is gone, Damien probably drugged and we're wasting precious time. Please."

Squire took in the woman before him, and again Damien picked up on something unspoken but clear as a bell. He felt something toward Beth, too. What though?

"Of course, follow me."

Beth and Moss on Squire's heels, while he and Trick lingered in the back. Smart kid. He was taking in all his surroundings, no doubt bookmarking anything he thought would be useful.

"So, dude, spill. What's the beef between you and these corn-fed boneheads?" Trick whispered once Squire and the others had gone further ahead.

"I don't know what you mean." Damien tried to downplay the kid's questions. Now wasn't the time and he wasn't use to sharing his feelings anyway.

"C'mon, aren't we past this? You can trust me, man. I caught the dope on how you wanted to rip Squire's throat out. The way you almost did Coyt's. Something has you on edge."

"I can honestly say I don't know." And that was true. He didn't know.

"Fine. But you don't trust these 'tards anymore than I do. Am I right, man?"

Yep, Trick was still observing and noting things like windows or more doors. If Damien had a little brother, deep down he suspected he would be a lot like this kid.

A buzzing saved him from answering the kid's twenty questions and their attentions turned toward a large set of double doors that opened at the end of the corridor.

Inside the room lights came alive in vast array of twinkling colors. Red, blue, and yellow all flickered life as monitors, motion sensors and control panels blinked furiously.

A few quick movements and their first question was answered. No, there hadn't been any monitors in the rooms, only those they'd detected in the hallways. At first, the tapes reflected only lonely corridors. Then, if you'd blinked, you would have missed it. Dark shadows appeared on the walls like ink blots with nobody around to make them.

"I've seen them before," Moss offered. "Back at Demetrius's cave, when I'd gone through Octavia's secret passageway. They're abominations created by Demetrius."

"Yeah, we ran into them as well that day," Beth agreed "What are they?" Squire asked in genuine curiosity and concern.

"Well, according to Demetrius, more swamp gas than actual beings."

"How is such a thing even possible?" Squire leaned closer to the monitor before him, stunned at the peculiar and menacing sight. The shadows left the walls and became silhouettes of men. Men who slid right through the door and into the room Grace and Damien had been given.

"With dark magic, I suppose nothing is off limits," Beth whispered, her fear and worry for Grace clear.

"Excuse me, I sensed the commotion from up here and wanted to check on what was happening."

They turned to find the woman named Red had appeared behind them. Odd Damien hadn't sensed another's presence. He should have, unless someone purposely cloaked their presence. Something again wasn't right that neither he, nor it appeared Moss, had been aware of her arrival. The more he thought about the peculiar woman, the more his gut skittered with unease. She bore no particular scent he could detect. Everyone, shifter or other, carried a unique scent.

"Yes, Red. I want you to head down and inform the others the compound was exposed last night. Find out if anyone sensed or heard anything wrong. Off. Maybe even just a small brownout or like."

"Sure thing, boss man, but can I ask what's happened?"

Damien maneuvered himself behind the woman and while for the most part his slight movements went unnoticed, a faint voice reached through the throbs of pain still lancing his head.

"What's going on? You're up to something. I can tell," Beth asked mentally.

"It seems our friend Red here is set on hiding something and I want to know what." He pushed the message around in his head not quite sure how this telepathic communication thing worked.

"How so?"

"She bears no scent. Everyone has a scent...It screams wrong." Once behind the woman, he took another whiff. Not even perfume,

deodorant or shampoo. Not one damn glandular scent wafted from the lying bitch. Nothing normal could possibly account for that, which only left magical. Why would a B.E.A.R. member need magical enhancements to cloak her scent, unless someone else's scent lingered on her she didn't want detected? *"Beth, be ready. My animal side has found a traitor."*

Out of the corner of his eye, he saw Red flip a small switch. He didn't know what it went to, but he'd bet it was some kind of alarm that had been turned off during the night and now she raced to reset before anyone noticed. He watched Beth's face scrunch up in concentration—sweat beaded from her forehead and her eyes closed. Her head was partially turned so that the others weren't aware of whatever it was she attempted. Only he was privy to the extreme in her expression and posture.

Before he had a chance to mentally ask what she attempted, the little hellcat launched across the room and straight on Red.

If they'd thought his attack on Coyt bad…well, hell, they hadn't seen anything yet.

Chapter Fourteen

A cracking sound resonated around the room, machines clattered as bodies hit and bounced from one metal contraption to another. Hair and curses flew madly about.

"Where the fuck is she, bitch?" Though Beth asked, she gave no time for Red to answer. Damien watched as Beth exploded, becoming a nearly uncontrollable powerhouse. He worried what may happen if her power unleashed into the fury it had during the battle with Octavia when Beth had nearly brought the cave in around them from the sheer force emitting from her.

Hair, spit, and curses flew as the coppery smell of blood permeated the security room, and unlike when he had Coyt by the throat, none of them stepped between the vicious fight before them. A tooth hit the floor and Damien sighed in relief when he caught Red spit a decent amount of blood before Beth surged onto her again. There was no way at the moment to split the women apart without the chance of hurting one or both.

"What in the hell is she doing?" Squire shouted, jumping out of his seat in front of the monitor. Moss whirled around before the man could make a step and blocked his path to the melee.

"Kick her big ass, Beth," Trick bellowed to his left and trained his eyes on Beth's every jab, kick and strike.

"I do not have a big ass!" Red spat glaring daggers of death at Trick.

"Bitch, backstabbing your own friends like that," Beth seethed. "You're going to wish your stank ass was never born." Beth yanked Red's head back so hard Damien was shocked the other woman's neck didn't snap. Her assault continued as she slammed Red's face down against the control board and continued doing so until blood spatter coated the console and another of Red's teeth went flying. Red kicked outward and sent Beth sprawling backward.

Sirens blared all around them and Squire shot them a menacing look demanding someone break the women up. Even knowing he had a traitor among his group of comrades, he couldn't stomach seeing one of his own pulverized.

Too fucking bad, Damien thought, relieved and glad Beth took matters into her own hands. He'd never lay a hand on a woman, but this traitor…well he'd have figured something out.

Heavy footsteps echoed down the hallway, coming in their direction and fast.

"You think you're better than everyone else, Barbie?" Red screeched gaining her footing on Beth.

"Who the fuck are you calling Barbie?" Beth zipped from the awkward posture she'd ended up in from Red's kick to her gut, and sailed past the hands that now blindly reached in between them in a vain attempt to rip the two apart.

Again, ill chosen timing did little to break the dueling duo up, but hell, he'd tried to tell Squire to back off.

"Damn, dude…you checking her bad self out? Beth's stomping Red a new ass, man." Trick didn't seem the slightest concerned for Beth. Truthfully none of them did as the minx ripped chunks of red hair while bashing Red's head against any hard surface she could. None of the men had any doubt of Beth's anger, but if they were to question the other gal, they needed to intercede. Squire sadly had a point. Beth made her statement, now Red needed to make hers.

"Beth. Easy honey, remember, she may be our only clue as to where Grace is." Moss interjected himself between the bodies and snatched Beth around her waist. Legs and arms flailed as she fought trying desperately to get back to the woman. "Easy, baby,"

Moss coxed doing his best to soothe his mate. Damien understood and commended his fierce loyalty to her. Beth proved passionate in all she did, including fighting for those she called her own. His friend indeed had scored a true treasure.

"Moss, let me go or so help me God…" she hissed, still spitting mad.

"Or you'll what, love?" Moss whispered something into her ear that settled her instantly. Her body relaxed into his, her breathing calmed and her posture returned to normal.

"Well, we wouldn't want that to happen." Damien caught her reply and slight blush as she calmed within his friend's embrace.

The rest of the B.E.A.R. members piled in to check what caused all the chaos and screaming that must have echoed through the building. Squire gave instructions for Red to be taken down into questioning. Damien didn't need to be told about the room to get the message it wasn't as hospitable as the other plush rooms within the compound.

"You are so going to pay for that, bitch. He's going to rain hell down around you and I'll be there to laugh as you scream," Red swore retribution on Beth.

"Bring it, Bozo." Damien caught the muscles in Moss's arm clench as he held Beth tight. She'd begun fighting to get free again.

Once Slick drug her away, Squire apologized for all the fucktardery that had transpired under his command.

"We'd suspected a mole within our group, but until now, I truly had no idea who'd be working for those monsters."

"How could you not have noticed what a carrot top bitch you had lurking around?" Beth was clearly still angry and wanting to lash out.

"Red's been with me since near the start. I'm clueless as to what they offered her to prompt a sudden switching of sides." Squire genuinely looked flustered and disappointed.

"She had feelings for you."

They all turned to find Bev standing quietly in the doorway.

"No. Impossible. If she did, she never said a word to me. Never even hinted." He scratched the top of his head.

"She did. You just never slowed down enough to notice. Never caught how she bent over in front of you, or how she made a point to sit near you each night."

He shook his head, still clearly not coming to grips with everything he'd missed right before his eyes.

"To hear her say it, you two were friends with benefits," Bev added.

Damien didn't miss the accusation and hurt on the other woman's face. Bev may not believe Red one hundred percent, but she suspected somewhere amid the traitor's tales lay a bit of truth. When Squire turned away from her, Damien winced. Apparently the truth had reared itself and bit him on his royal ass. Problem Damien had with the man's lie was the fact Squire's truth screwed Grace over in bad way.

"None of this gets us any closer to finding Grace. Let me drill the scorned lover," he said impatiently. Anger made him toss that dig of his own in Squire's direction. Which earned him a narrowed gaze from the man. A warning. Too bad Damien viewed warnings as challenges, nothing more.

"No. You won't be able to play dirty enough. The fact she's a woman will hold you back. I'm the best choice to drill her." Beth jumped at the chance to question Red again.

"While I appreciate your willingness, I'm putting Bev and Lily in charge." Squire nodded at Bev, who disappeared he assumed to get whoever Lily was.

"Fine, but we stand in as well. And if we're not satisfied with what this woman has to say, we step in," Damien threatened, not at ease with the call, but willing to give them one shot at getting the answers he needed.

"Fair enough. Follow me downstairs to the cellar." Squire stood and headed for the elevators. Damien stayed in control for the most part, but knowing Demetrius had Grace in his clutches kept him unsettled. Nothing would ease the ache stabbing his heart except having Grace safe in his embrace again.

Even before they'd entered the room, Damien's sensitive hearing picked up the fast flowing threats launched at that Lily person. Squire opened a massive steel door and a surgical-like room presented itself. Everything in the room was pristine, clean, sparkling, sterling silver.

Dead center of the room, tied to a large chair, sat one very pissed off Red.

"Where is Grace?" Damien may have agreed to hold back, but his need for swift answers overtook the promise.

"Where you will never find her," Red spat in their direction. Hatred dripped from her every pore.

"Pity for you in that case," Bev said simply. So softly spoken and unchallenging, Red took the bait.

"And why is that, Bev? If you ask me, more like pity for them." Red nodded her head in their direction. Damien's eyes narrowed and though his mind warned against striking a woman, his beast swore no woman sat before him. Only a monster who wished harm against his mate.

"Oh, but I disagree. Know why? Because you were willing to prove your love and where are you now? Sitting here, tied up, and taking the rap. And what did Demetrius do? Forsake your love by having you help him steal the only woman he wants. Loves. Boy that's gotta sting. I'd be pissed. Livid in fact." Bev hopped up and slid back on one of the numerous countertops in the room, crossed her legs and continued. "I mean. He loves her, you love him…but unlike Demetrius, you ran around doing all the dirty work. You're the one who got caught. And where is he? I don't think anyone's outside pounding on our front door to get you back. It's called expendable and is your new title."

"Fuck you. He'll come. Just you wait. But unlike Demetrius, will Squire ever come after you? Or will you continue to pine for him from darkened corners? Oh yeah. I've watched you, Bev. Seen you drool as he passes by. Recognized the burn from experience, didn't you? Must really chap your ass Squire spent his nights in my bed, rather than yours."

Damien grew concerned when the color drained from Bev's face and he prayed the woman held her shit together. Red had become rattled when Bev was on the attack, and he hoped this woman could continue doing so. Unnerved meant Red might slip up and give away Grace's or Demetrius's location.

"Oh priceless. You should see your face. And you," Red's attention swiveled toward Squire. "have led her on. Led me on for a while as well. I'll own my mistakes, but mind you, Demetrius isn't one of them. You, on the other hand…does Damien know of your special connection with Grace?"

"It's a private matter between Grace and myself, no other."

Damien cleared his throat. Squire was dead wrong if he thought anything he had with Grace would be private. Damien's first priority was getting Grace back safe and sound. But if this man, Squire, thought he wouldn't be involved in anything going down between Grace and his self…well, he was sorely mistaking.

"Please, Red. Grace has done nothing to you and if you truly love Demetrius, why not help us get her back? Away from him. So he will want and need you again?"

They turned their attention on the mousy girl that until now had remained library quiet.

"I'm sorry, Lily. I really did like you, sweetie, but I can't do that. What I will say is they are coming after you next. I know how you hate them, so I'm warning you now. I owe you that much." Red's eyes softened a tad while she spoke to the girl.

"If you really wanted to help, tell us where the innocent is." Lily again addressed Red without glancing at any others. "I don't want to hurt you. Please don't make me."

"You? Hurt me? On what planet, halfling?" Red laughed openly, her tussle of red curls shaking as she did.

In less than a second, Red began keening loudly in obvious distress. Her hands bound to the chair gnarled in arthritic proportions and her knees drew inward, an instinct to rock away the pain. She paled, gagging as tears streamed down her face. Her breaths came in short pain-filled pants until finally whatever the hell hit her passed.

"Please answer our questions. I don't want to have to dig around again."

Lily had done something. Damien studied the young woman. From all outward appearances, she appeared no older than her late teens or early twenties, was of slim build. For all intents and purposes, not someone who jumped out at you. Until you caught sight of her soulful brown eyes. Therein lay her beauty.

Right now Lily's eyes filled with unshed tears over what she warned she must do.

"Please, Red. Turn the bad around. Think of another, rather than yourself," Lily pleaded and Damien gathered she and Red must have been tight at one time.

Red panted so hard her bangs blew up and down off her sweat-covered forehead, leaving a few strands stuck in the dewed mess.

"I can't. He'll—kill—me—if I do," she barely rasped through the radiating pain that seemed to still be assailing her.

"If you don't, we will," Damien said, walking over to lean over in front of the woman. His peripheral vision picked up Squire edging closer. Good. The man didn't know what he'd do, or not do, and that worked to Damien's advantage. "Unlike the others, I won't apologize for the pain I inflict. I take care of me and mine, and right now you are the threat to them I intend to neutralize. Be it long and painful or short and sweet. Your call."

"If you kill me you'll never find her." Yeah, Red tried for brave, but the stutter in her voice told him she was far from it. Their little rat was reconsidering which side her furry ass was buttered on.

"If you don't help us, I don't see I have anything to lose in extinguishing a threat. Do you?" He was nose to nose with her and when she finally braved looking upward and caught his glare, he saw her decision before she even spoke it.

"Don't lie, Red, I reviewed enough in your mind to know whether you are speaking the truth," Lily threatened.

"And if they don't kill you for lying, you will wish they did by the time I get done with you," Beth promised, inching closer to Red herself.

"In the dark. They have her in the dark." Red started crying openly. Her entire body shook in defeat and, no doubt, fear.

"What the hell does that mean? In the dark?" Damien growled, shaking the woman so hard her teeth clattered together. "Tell us now, damn you."

Squire grabbed him by the shoulders and pulled him back. "Ease up, friend. She's already agreed to tell us." Damien sensed the other man wasn't the least bit upset that he'd shaken Red, but rather had a good cop, bad cop plan. "Why don't you wait over there with your friend?" He motioned to where Trick stood.

A slight nod assured him the questioning was far from over. Merely different tactics.

"I've told you already. She's in the dark." Exhausted, Red glanced at Lily, who nodded her head at Squire that she spoke the truth.

"Where would this dark be exactly?" Squire accepted a damp cloth from Bev and proceeded to wipe the cool comfort across Red's forehead.

"I never saw but…"

"But what?"

"Demetrius smelled kinda funny when he got back from dropping her off wherever he's hiding her."

"Funny like how?"

"Like death."

Chapter Fifteen

Grace awoke slowly with a nasty medicinal taste in her mouth. *Ugh.* She sat up and grabbed her head. *Damn, how much did I drink last night?* Then remembered, none. She hadn't even gone out. Damien had been curled around her and she'd been the most relaxed she'd been in weeks.

So how the hell did I end up here? Where was here and why does the weird aroma seem so hauntingly familiar?

The room around her was rather dark and the lounge she lay across covered in crushed velvet. A few moments later her eyesight adjusted to the dim surroundings and her heart stuck in her throat. All around her sat caskets. Some opened, some shut, but all most certainly caskets.

As if that weren't creepy enough, a light methodic melody played on speakers anchored in the corners of the room.

Standing on wobbly legs, Grace eased her way over to the opened black box and relief soared when she discovered only satin fabric and no dead body. Grabbing the lid to the next one, her heart stuttered as the creaky lid opened. Empty. After verifying all were vacant of new owners, the realization she woke up in a funeral home showroom sank in. How the hell did she go to sleep nestled safe and secure in Damien's arms, only to awake in this God awful place?

Honestly she didn't know which was worse. All the coffins or the too clean, too powdery scent. Then the music stopped and everything became deathly silent. *Creepy.*

"Hello, Grace, I see that you've finally awakened. I trust you had a decent sleep."

Oh fuck a duck. Demetrius.

"Bed was a bit lumpy, but yes. Slept like the dead." Everything in her to refused to show fear. Yeah, he freaked her the fuck out, but he damn well wasn't going to know.

"Ah, very good then. I've taken the liberty to plan the day for us. First dates are so important. First impressions and all. Don't you agree?"

She'd agree he was a complete fruitcake. Boy, did she hate that overrated Christmas gift. Not as much as Demetrius though.

"Well, I hadn't expected you to be too chatty yet. If I may draw your attention to the shelves over in the far corner. Yes, the ones housing the urns. On the third rack you will find several boxes. Consider them gifts to show my affection for you."

"You know I'm super cranky in the mornings. Look like shit actually. Oh and I suffer terrible flatulence. You should find a better girlfriend. Less gas, more glitter."

"Enjoy the gifts, Grace. Oh and I expect you dressed and ready within the hour. I'd hate for us to get off on the wrong foot."

A click resonated around the small room when the speaker shut off. Grace sprang for the only door in the room and tested its strength. Fuck. Solid wood. Taking a few steps backwards, she ran full steam and threw her body into the door. She bounced right off, landing unceremoniously on her ass.

Shit, shit, shit. She massaged her throbbing shoulder and surveyed the door. *Not even a damn crack.*

Well hell. Sprawled on her ass on the floor wouldn't help anything. She glanced toward the boxes he mentioned and supposed she should prepare for her meeting with Demetrius. Maybe he really was as stupid as he seemed and she could play this out to her advantage. Convince him she'd had a change in heart. Show some interest in him or his organization.

Before her on the shelf sat numerous elaborately wrapped gifts. She gathered the shiny bowed packages and took a seat back on the lounge she woke up on to carefully peel back the paper as she feared what may be inside. The man was insane. Unwrapping a heart or bloodied hand would gross her out, but she wouldn't be shocked. Her nail scored under the tape holding the lid down and she held her breath—and her stomach.

Royal blue silken fabric. An elegant dress met her wary gaze. Nervous, yet relieved, she grabbed the next box. A matching pair of stilettos. Had this been Christmas, she'd be cursed at for moving so damn slow. But one couldn't be too cautious when opening gifts from a lunatic. The other gifts held a sapphire necklace, earrings, and the matching bracelet. She thought herself past any shock. But sadly the final wrapped box held a humdinger.

Thigh highs, a royal blue thong and a matching push-up demi bra. Shudders racked her at thoughts of the pervert picking out lingerie for her. Glancing up at the clock on the wall, she was down to thirty-five minutes before the designated time he'd given her. Crap. Unsure of her choice yet, she paced the room.

Play along with him or look for weapons? Surely there had to be something in the room he'd missed removing or putting up away from her. A small credenza stood over in another corner of the room. Racing over she yanked on the doors, scavenging through each drawer looking for anything that might be used against him.

Argh. Not a damn thing even resembling a weapon.

Each drawer housed literature on the different type of caskets and urns the funeral home offered. Not even a damn pen worthy of jabbing his eyes out turned up.

Guess that answered whether she would play along or fight back. Unless a pillow fight with satin pillows counted, nothing else lay around. She eyed the heel of the stiletto but knew to make the shoe count as a deadly weapon she'd have to get up close and personal and that would be far too risky.

Time to gussy herself up she supposed, fighting but not succeeding in suppressing another shudder at the prospect.

With a heavy sigh, she removed Damien's shirt, lingering when the fabric passed her nose. The mere scent of her shifter brought tears to her eyes. Even if he'd already begun scouring the earth to find her, she didn't even recognize where she was confined. Prayed wherever Demetrius took her for the "date" would provide an opportunity for escape. Rubbing the fabric against her cheek one last time, Grace hoped Damien's unique male scent would linger and piss Demetrius off.

Oh my God. Why didn't I think of this sooner?

Not wanting to stand around naked, she slipped the dress on. The cool fabric, which normally would have created a luxurious sensation, only created terror as it slid against her naked skin. Once clothed, she brought Damien's shirt to her face again and breathed in his smell while mentally sending a message.

Damien, I'm being held in a funeral home.

She ran back to the literature drawer. Damn. What company didn't promote their name on their brochures? Oh. All the pamphlets were from the casket manufacturers and not the actual funeral home. Double damn.

Damien…if you can hear me try to think me something. Concentrate really hard. Damien might not be telepathic, but she was. All he had to do was concentrate on broadcasting his thoughts while thinking of her.

Glancing at the clock again, she realized she was down to twenty minutes before Demetrius arrived. Not wanting to chance dressing in front him, especially putting on the underwear, bra, and thigh highs, she continued sending Damien mental thoughts of her surroundings. The pale blue walls, dark wood furniture and even a possible date the building was constructed Though having seen only the room where she now stood, she had no doubts this building or house was old. Like historical kind of old.

Once she'd wiggled into the under things and slid the sheers into place, she slipped the heels on and waited. Impatient and nervous, she fidgeted with her hands in her lap. Then she got up and paced. Minutes later she returned to the lounger and fidgeted again.

The sound of metal on metal stopped her wiggling and her heart. A key was turning the lock.

Demetrius had arrived and the time for second thoughts long over. She steeled herself to do whatever necessary to survive and prayed with everything in her Damien had received her message. Wasn't a lot, but she knew her shifter was crafty and had a sense of smell that put a bloodhound's to shame. He'd find her. He had to.

"I knew the blue would look stunning on you. And the fit. Please stand and do a little turn. Isn't that what women like, showing off their goods?"

His crass comments disturbed her, but she hadn't expected anything more from him.

She stood on legs she willed steady and did a slow turn, schooling her face devoid of emotion for when she faced him again.

"Yes. Simply lovely. Are you ready for a day filled with surprises?"

"Do I have a choice?"

"No, I'm afraid you don't. But how well our day goes depends entirely on you. I would suggest you remember that and make the most of my gracious nature. When you sprinted around the room looking for I assume a weapon, I grew worried. But then you surprised me and changed."

Grace swallowed the bile that rose. "You spied on me changing. Doesn't seem like a gentlemanly thing to do."

"No, I suppose not. However I didn't think you'd leave me much choice. But let's put the unpleasantries behind us. You changed your mind as is a woman's prerogative so let's move forward now."

He didn't need to add the or else, it was there. The unspoken, underlying threat.

"Very well. May I at least inquire as to where we are going?"

"Oh and spoil the surprise? I think not."

Demetrius came her way she assumed to lead her out, but no. He came nearly nose to nose and his gaze dipped to her cleavage. He didn't even bother pretending he wasn't ogling. Worse, she knew he'd already seen everything.

"My dear, haven't you forgotten something?"

Her stomach threatened to revolt as she feared he wanted a kiss…and relief washed over her when instead he leaned past her to pick up the jewelry box. She'd forgotten to put on the sapphires he'd given her.

"Turn around." A quiet demand.

Grace hated turning her back to him but did as he instructed. Better to keep him happy. At least for now.

"Lift your hair for me, darling."

Again she followed his orders and bit back her retort at his endearment. She was not his fucking darling. Not now, not ever.

She belonged to Damien.

Even thinking it calmed her. Gave her the strength she needed for whatever he'd planned.

"Now there we are. Perfect. The icing atop the cherry. Oh my. Rather backwards, but suitable I believe. Yes?" He still stood behind her. So close she felt the heat from his breath on the back of her neck and refused to think about the thing poking her in the small of her back. He damn well better have his phone in his pocket.

Not trusting the words that might tumble forth, Grace took the safe road and nodded instead.

"Yes well. I believe we are ready for our adventure now." Demetrius took her arm at her elbow and ushered her toward the door. She sought the front door the minute they'd cleared the threshold to the room, formulating immediate plans to bolt.

Shit. Bastard had her blocked in at every turn. The ass actually had guard shadows?

"Yes. Pretend they aren't here, my sweet." Demetrius walked right past the two inky shadow figures standing outside the door. Since he seemed determined to play Mr. Sweet and Accommodating right now, she decided maybe she could learn a few things.

"So, not trying to be rude or anything, but exactly what are they?" The figures had the outer shape of a man, but no true substance. The closest description had she needed to describe them would be if someone dumped ink over the invisible man. The outline stood solid, but nothing else.

"They are my creations. Not my mother's, but those I bore." He beamed from pride.

Moss had nailed his assumptions of Demetrius. A cocky son of a bitch with clear mommy issues. Well his mommy died, so the asshat's excuse was gone.

"How, uh, creative. Now, exactly who are they?" No way could she keep the sarcasm from her voice.

"Not who. You were right the first time. What."

"I'm biting. What are they?" she pushed.

"Swamp gas."

She tripped on the small lip of one of the stepping stones lining the front walk. "Did you just say swamp gas?"

"Yes. They possess no human DNA within their matter. They cannot be killed or harmed, should you think of trying to escape. Which I would urge you not to try. I'd like today to memorable. In a good way, that is."

Jackass thought today wouldn't be memorable? Hello, kidnapped by a mad scientist ranked in things she doubted she'd ever forget.

She turned and saw the vehicle before her. He had to be kidding. *A hearse? Seriously?*

"Ah, here we are." When he opened the back door, she saw seating rather than the open space a casket would require. Obviously he'd had the thing customized. The man had some serious head issues.

He slid in next to her, the silver threads in his black hair glinting in afternoon sunlight. If not for his beady eyes and puny size, he may have been considered distinguished looking by some. But she was all about the eyes, and his held a madness within the squinty glare. Once she'd settled, she noted the absence of ink people getting in the front seat.

"Do not fear. Marcus and Gregor are my miracles, but even I wouldn't allow them to drive. Lark is my driver." At the end of his statement the window separating the backseat from front lowered until the driver's cap became visible.

But while her stomach settled in appreciation that a living, breathing person would be driving them, the thought struck.

Wasn't swamp gas highly combustible?

Chapter Sixteen

Leaning over he put his head in his hands. The whole dark and smelled like death had been too much. His temples throbbed as a strange dizziness swept through him. The sensation of needles stabbing his brain began right before visual snippets hit him. A house. Plush carpet. Old wooden doors. The fragmented images coming in short spurts.

What the hell?

Grace! For one second, he could actually smell her as strong as if she were in his arms. His body tingled, his animal shot to high alert and a few more images came through before the link vanished. His heart stopped when her scent did.

Damien stared out the window before shutting his eyes and bringing her image to the forefront of his mind. Did his damndest to mentally send a return message to Grace, to hold on. Stay strong. Stay smart, he would find her. That he'd received her descriptions of the funeral home and of the black hearse with black stallion hood ornament on the front. He didn't know how the hell telepathy worked, but gave it his all and prayed.

He relayed to the others what happened and everyone sprang to action.

Trick's lame ass had asked if he'd gotten constipated. He'd have to have a talk with the kid when this shit was all over, but ripping the punk a new one would have to wait.

"Has she sent anymore messages or image locations?" Squire's voice was deep. The concern and familiarity with Grace, was quite clear and still pissing him off.

They'd sent Moss and Beth in one direction and Trick and Lily in another, all driving around looking for the strange hearse. Everyone had their cell phones charged and on. Trick jumped at the chance to ride with Lily, the intention behind his actions evident in the boner the kid kept getting every time the girl was near. Which left him stuck with Squire. Of course the dilemma did leave him with an opportunity to determine just how this man knew Grace.

His Grace. He had a hard time wrapping his mind around the thought. He'd been alone so long he wasn't sure anyone, let alone Grace, could survive his quirks. Would he be able to survive hers?

"Quit, that's irritating as fuck," Squire commented, and Damien realized he'd been thumping the dash with his fingers while lost in thought.

He'd have time to figure that out later. Right now the only thing he understood with certainty was that he couldn't tolerate any other male around her. Should she not want him, least not as a mate, he'd deal with the fact then. Until he knew for sure, Squire better steer the fuck away from her.

"So, how do you know Grace?"

"What makes you think I do?"

"Don't play me for the fool. We haven't time to spare for bullshit."

"Wouldn't it be far more prudent if you concentrated on receiving a message should she send another?" Squire continued driving and avoiding his question. But his knuckles had gone white on the steering wheel.

"I'll know if she sends one. Now answer the question." Damien's patience had run out. This man poised a serious threat to he and Grace. He sensed a competitor but wanted to understand why.

"When we get Grace safely back, I'll explain. Until we do, and I can speak privately with her, you're shit out luck. Don't like it, I can pull over and let you out." Squire left little room to argue and as much as Damien's instincts hummed to neutralize the threat, namely Squire, he couldn't. Too much stood to chance with rescuing Grace. The more eyes scouring for her, the better. Not to mention they were in Squire's vehicle. A four-wheel drive bulky guy car no less. A freaking Hummer. Damien thought of other hummers he'd have wanted more and from whom.

Pretty green grass…poles. Clean scent. Flags. Big bulletin boards with words…or numbers.

"She sent something else." He blurted out what she'd shown him including the smell, to the best he could describe, before he called Beth on speakerphone.

"Beth, she sent more," he spat, sounding curt but unable to change the anxiety building.

"What did you see?"

"A green manicured lawn cut short. I caught a glimpse of a big board with numbers or something. The place seemed familiar, but Jesus…I can't…wait! A golf course. Are any courses or clubs near funeral homes?"

"I can do a Google map search. Trick's running one now on hearses or funeral homes who use stallions as their logo. Give me five and I'll call you back."

"I vaguely remember a funeral home that fits the description, but I've been out of the loop for so long I can't remember where." Squire slammed his fist into the steering wheel and the Hummer swerved off road a minute.

A mere moment, but what seemed an eternity later, Beth called.

"We're pretty sure we've got a lock on their location. The Swamp Lair Country Club. The place is a pretty exclusive, members only kind of thing, and the closest establishment happens to be a funeral home named Derbyshire Manor. That has to be where they are, Damien."

Her caught the desperation in Beth's voice. Understood her panic. One hundred percent.

"I agree. Let me give Squire the directions and we'll meet you guys at the club. Stay outside the main entrance though. I don't want to spook him and give him any reason to endanger Grace."

The Hummer's tires squealed as Squire peeled out in a U-turn to head back from the direction they came. Man had to be hitting close to a hundred and Damien had no complaints. The faster the better.

His phone went off again.

"Dude, we got the message. Lily and I'll be there to back you guys up. I know, meet outside the gate. Beth already told me."

Damien picked up Lily's voice in the background. Sounded like the mousy girl had grown quite chatty while with Trick.

The rest of his ride was in awkward silence. Damien got the feeling he was being sized up. Fine with him. He and Squire would be squaring off soon.

And damned if he wasn't looking forward to it.

• • •

"Veal Marsala, roasted red potatoes and peppers, steamed asparagus, and port wine. For dessert I took the liberty of ordering crème brûlée." Demetrius pulled out the little white wooden chair from the table, which sat dead center on a golf course. She'd read the club sign on the way in and did her best to send the mental image of its name to Damien. Once they'd arrived, their driver remained with the hearse and Gregor and Marcus, or ink blot number one and ink blot number two, shadowed them, pun intended, to their table.

If she wasn't mistaken, crème brûlée came flaming, or at the least was flamed tableside. If she was lucky, this exclusive club had a chef. One who would prepare the dish as it was meant to be served.

"Actually that sounds wonderful." At least on the current topic of conversation she could be truthful. If he stayed on the conversation, stalling him until the others arrived, or the dessert did, left her with a decent shot at escape.

"I know we may have gotten off on the wrong foot, but I assure you. I'm not the cad you believe me to be."

Damn, but if Demetrius didn't take a header off the safe topic bridge. Even he wouldn't have been stupid enough if she jumped and agreed everything had been a misunderstanding. Wrong foot? Hell, more like two left feet kind of wrong. Playing it safe, she simply nodded.

"After my mother's death, the society deemed me best suited to head the committee governing them. Most of the members are so old school stuffy, they wouldn't be able to find their way out of a breadbox in broad daylight." He shook his head as if completely baffled by the prospect. "They refuse to acknowledge the way of the future and insist upon keeping to the standards set by our forefathers. Quite unnecessarily barbaric."

"You don't say." Damn, the quip slid off her tongue before she'd been able to prevent the slippage.

"Please don't go and ruin our afternoon by being crass." He forced direct eye contact and the serious set of his gaze alerted her he meant business. "I can be your ally or your enemy and the choice is entirely yours. However, I should add that if you choose to remain willingly by my side, I will assure the safety of your friends. So long as they don't attack us, I will not go after them. Consider this another gift."

"How can I even begin to tell them not to go after you? You people nearly destroyed their lives." Her voice rose and the inky men drew closer until a flick of Demetrius's hand stayed them.

"I'm sure you can be convincing under the right circumstances." He slid another wrapped box across the table. "Go ahead and open your gift now." Something in his voice threatened that whatever the box held would not be like the baubles he'd bestowed on her earlier.

Hands shaking, she gently unwrapped the shiny threat. Within the package was a small black box with blinking red light.

"Understand that even as we speak, there is bomb placed in the head of B.E.A.R.'s vehicle. You'd be surprised how easy hiding a bomb on a Hummer is."

Her gut sank. Grace prayed he bluffed. If nothing else, prayed Damien rode with one of the others. If she lost her shifter... Tears threatened to spill. Again the swamp threatened to take what she loved. First Henry, now Damien.

No! Fuck that. This asshat was going down. She fingered the box as delicately as one would a sugar sculpture with wet hands.

"I give you the box to prove you control their fate. Not I. Give me your word you will remain at my side, and nothing will happen to your friends. And Grace, I will know if you're lying."

Without batting an eye, she said, "I give you my word." And she did. He didn't specify for how long. If she killed him, she would have still, technically, remained at his side.

Demetrius studied her a moment. Stared her directly in the eyes before thankfully nodding his approval and placing his napkin in his lap as if threatening others' lives were but an entree to his main course.

Grace kept the box close. She wasn't sure if he'd intended to disengage it then or later, and she damn sure didn't want any accidents. Doing her best, she sent a mental image of the box. Demetrius stared so intently, she feared he somehow figured out what she was doing. But if so, he made no mention or move to stop her.

Lunch arrived, saving her from further conversation and during a moment when he turned away to take a phone call while covering the mouth piece with his hand, she stashed the knife that accompanied her meal under her thigh. He turned back, but not in time to see her pocket the weapon. Immobilizing Demetrius wouldn't be her problem. Doing so while snatching the torch from the chef, if her plan worked out, would be the tricky part.

"You've barely touched your meal. Is something wrong with your food?" He snapped his fingers and moments later a man cruised up on a golf cart. The chef no doubt.

"No, no the food is wonderful. I'm just not a very big eater and wanted to save room for the decadent dessert you mentioned earlier." She rubbed her stomach for good measure in such a way she hoped convinced him she was eagerly anticipating the dessert coming.

"Very well. Marshall, our guest is ready for her sweets. Please prepare her dish now."

Now or never. Sadly, if she fucked up, it wasn't only her ass on the line. She'd be responsible for who knew how many deaths. And Damien's.

Failing was *not* an option.

Marshall, their chef, set about the dishes and ingredients required to make the famous dish. She slid the box under the table and hoped the old adage "out of sight, out of mind" rang true. The moment the chef rounded the table to Demetrius's side, she snatched the knife she'd hidden and slammed it into Demetrius's hand, which rested flat on the table. The chef, being a man of intelligence, turkey necked himself backward from the melee. The man even had the good sense to take off in the opposite direction. The two ink blots charged her as she suspected they'd do, and grabbing the cooking torch, she pulled the lever. The flame erupted to life as the dark duo converged on her.

Just as she'd suspected, they combusted in an eruption of red and blue foul-smelling flames. The heat scorched her face though she jumped as far away as possible from the volatile flames and stench. Damn but swamp gas stunk.

Because she'd been so close, her leap hadn't been as quick as she'd hoped. The hem of her dress caught fire. She rolled in frantic fashion about the ground trying to put the burning fabric out. Intent and frazzled at being on fire, she never heard the yowl of pain or saw Demetrius as he yanked the steak knife out of his hand. Nor did the sight of his disappearance under the table come to light until she'd put out her smoldering dress and sat up.

Then she saw him. Noted what held and screamed when he pushed the flashing button on the bomb's mechanism.

The explosion was immediate and close. Plumes of black smoke billowed from the entrance of the club. Time froze. Sounds went silent as an odd ringing started. Small and so faint at first but gaining momentum. Grace didn't recognize what she listened to. But after a second of looking around, she realized the humming-like sound came from within.

The ground rumbled beneath her prone body and the world went into slow motion. When her eyes locked on Demetrius, she knew the moment the man began to fear. But it was too late. He'd started a sequence of events not even she could undo. Even as awareness settled and the carnage began, she didn't attempt to stop it. With Damien's image in her mind and Demetrius before her, she embraced the dark weaving itself within her magic…and her soul.

Chapter Seventeen

They pulled up to the gates within minutes of the others. Moss played hell holding Beth back from storming in blind. As for Trick and Lily, something seemed to be sparking between the two. Trick so much as looked in her direction and the girl went beet red. But both appeared standing shoulder to shoulder ready for battle.

Squire got out and came around to join him as Damien leaned over the hood of Hummer, reviewing the layout of the course on Squire's electronic tablet contraption. To him the thing looked like nothing more than a glorified cell phone on steroids. The squared object lit up and after a few taps from Squire, a map popped up showing the entire grounds of the club including the clubhouse, the parked golf carts and the gym that housed the sauna, pool and showering area."I'd assume he'd have her in the clubhouse. That's where the dining and guest rooms are." Squire stabbed at the dot on the map indicating the guest lodge.

The thought of Grace with Demetrius in a guest room soured his meal from the night before. Images of what Demetrius may be doing to Grace flooded Damien's mind before he could stop them. Grace's silk-like skin, bared and flushed. Nipples peaked and begging for attention. He nearly drooled as the memory of their lovemaking overtook him. The way her rose-colored buds stiffened in his mouth as he suckled and tongued them. Demetrius taking liberties with the body that had bloomed for him brought bubbling rage. Damien's vision tunneled as the anger released the animal within. Everything zeroed in on simple, primal levels. No need for thoughts of laws, right or wrong. Only survival of he and his. His fists opened and closed, knuckles cracked, and Squire took a step back.

"Keep your shit together. We can't afford anyone going in half-cocked and chancing her life."

Squire was right, but he'd bypassed the time for reasoning when the vision of Demetrius fucking Grace rolled to mind.

Calm. Imagine the beach. Or snow or swamp. Whatever or wherever you find solace in.

Lily. How the girl spoke in his head so loud and clear remained a pure mystery. Grace managed to get through, but not with the frequency or strength as the girl did.

I didn't mean to intrude, but I sensed your level of distress. You won't be of any help to Grace in the shape you are in.

Damien stepped away from them all. Took deep calming breaths and forced a wall of stability between his imagination and reality. Made himself hold back his fears and deal only with factual information. Grace was here, alive and everything else but a rumor in his overactive worrisome mind.

"Thank you," he whispered to Lily, who, for the first time since he'd laid eyes on the girl, beamed. He also noted the protective stance Trick took standing next to her. Kid actually had a challenging look in his eyes.

Grace was trying to send another message, but the image was so hazy Damien was unable to make out what she tried to relay.

A boom sounded right before a burn tore into his side. His ears pounded so hard he feared they bled. Everything around him went bright and hot. So fucking hot. He heard screams, the sounds of shattering glass and the odd tune of twisting metal. Nothing made sense, but instinct had him diving low for cover.

When the roll finished, he was on all fours behind Trick and Lily's borrowed vehicle. The sounds of sobs reached him, as did the strange observation that his sleeve was tattered and blood covered his arm. His other was a replica. Both arms reflected blood spatter, deep lacerations and charred sleeves.

"Beth…Moss…you guys okay?" He prayed they answered.

"We're fine, only scratches…but Trick doesn't look so good," Beth yelled but her voice ended on an odd grunt. Damien peeped over the top of Trick's vehicle and found Moss laying across her pinning her down and reprimanding her for bolting up out in the open like she did.

Damien laid flat on his belly and crawled military style to where he came across Lily crying.

"Thanks, I'm fine, too." He caught the sarcasm in Squire's tone, but he didn't really give a shit if he hurt the guy's feelings. Truthfully he was pissed the ass had even survived.

His hands hit warm puddles of something, and as he came around he found Lily cradling Trick's head in her lap and saw a large piece of metal sticking out from his belly. Her tears streamed as she attempted to comfort the kid. Shit. A belly wound like his didn't bode well at all.

"Squire, you called for backup yet?"

"On their way."

"Don't suppose you guys have a medic on staff?" He prayed they did, because Trick needed one here pronto. He tore a strip of his shirt off and ran it around the jagged metal. He couldn't chance removing the piece of Hummer for fear the kid would bleed out before help arrived, but they needed at minimum to stanch the blood flow.

"Don't press, but apply slight pressure. We just need to slow the flow until help arrives. Understand?" Lily nodded, looking terrified.

"Can you make out anyone?" Damien yelled concerned they were still being watched.

"No," came the reply from Squire. Things were quiet—of course now his hearing sounded muted, like in a tunnel.

"Damn you, Moss, lemme go," Beth screeched, and Damien saw her pushing frantically against his friend.

"Squire—stay with them while I try to find Grace." The man started to argue, but Lily called him to her side. Fear rode high with them all, but right now the girl appeared in near shock as she rocked the now unconscious Trick back and forth while mumbling something even Damien's excellent hearing couldn't make out enough to understand.

He raced from cover, scenting the air. If Grace were close, he'd be able to detect her fragrance. Finally a putrid smell of swamp gas, charred earth and a hint of Grace registered. He followed the odor, noting the grass turning from green to brown to ash black. A table had been overturned and shattered dishes littered the ground. As did what appeared to be the remnants of a man. Pieces of him lay scattered about, but most unusual was the fact it appeared more mummified than burned. Like a shriveled slug whose life got sucked out.

Though her scent lingered, he found no trace of Grace. At this particular spot, nearly the entire course was visible.

A clanking dish jerked him around, fist raised and ready.

"Where is she? I don't see her." The shrill tone told Damien Beth stood on the verge of an emotional breakdown as she heaved in deep gulping breaths, no doubt having run the whole way.

"I don't know. She was here though. I scented her."

He followed Beth's gaze to the gore on the ground before Moss came up from behind her and turned her away from remains. "Uh, who do you suppose the fritter is?" Moss asked while Beth began gagging.

"It isn't Grace. The smell signifies Demetrius."

"Well then where is Grace?"

"That's a damn good question," Squire said, walking up behind them.

Chapter Eighteen

They regrouped at B.E.A.R. Everyone was aggravated, stressed and worried. Grace didn't answer her phone, if she even still had the thing on her, which they all doubted. Trick was in surgery and by the nurses' and doctors' whispered comments and expressions at the ER, not doing very well.

Deflated. Summarized how Damien described them.

What had been set as a rescue mission turned into a nightmare of epic proportions. Between the bomb, Grace's disappearance and the unusual condition of Demetrius's body, everyone felt clueless what to think.

Lily wanted to stay by Trick's side, but Squire worried that given her current emotional state, which they deemed unstable at best, doing so too risky. Last thing anyone needed to happen was for unexplained events to plague the hospital, drawing attention to the supernatural battle at hand. Damien agreed wholeheartedly the best situation was to stay hidden. Moss wasn't keen on coming out of the closet about being a reptile shifter anymore than he wanted to be outed as an armadillo shifter.

"What the hell happened? And if Grace is the one who pulverized Demetrius, where is she? Maybe Demetrius didn't act alone in her kidnapping. She did mention the strange mystery voice she heard who claimed the society viewed her as a threat due to Demetrius feelings for her. Could they have been watching and swooped in and taken her?" Beth asked appearing drawn and fragile.

Before Damien could reply, someone else did.

"I was the voice she heard at her shop." Lily stood before them, eyes red and swollen yet her posture straight and proud. "I couldn't let them win. I've still a friend within their group. It's too risky for her to tell me everything, but when she thinks it's safe or if the situation is grave enough, she sends me alerts."

The slip, *I still have friends* hadn't gone unnoticed. "And how are you connected to the society?" Damien crossed his arms over his still bare chest.

"She was Demetrius's daughter." Squire announced in a monotone, matter of fact manner. Like they all should just be peachy with.

They whirled around to gape at Squire. He'd entered and gone to stand next to Lily, putting his arm around her and tossing Damien a clean t-shirt. "Thought you might like a change." Squire continued as if not having just dropped a bombshell.

"Come again?" Beth's voice hit shrill notes and shot even further. "How can we be sure Lily's not in on whatever the hell happened?"

"My father was evil, my grandmother evil, but my mother? She hadn't a mean bone in her body. She merely made the mistake of falling in love with the wrong man. Around the time I turned eight, she snatched me out of my bed in the middle of the night and we ran," the young girl defended herself.

"Surely Octavia nor Demetrius would simply let you go without hunting to the ends of the earth." Seeing how distraught she was tore Damien in two, but Grace's life hung in the balance.

"They didn't. They tracked us down a few years later and drug us back. They locked us in a room, and the next day ripped me from my mother's arms and led her away. I never laid eyes on her again. Five years later Squire kidnapped me, and explained the situation as best he could to a precocious ten-year-old that life would be happy and safe here with him. They were friends of my mother's and her last wish was for them to take care of me."

Damien caught the look Beth gave him. She didn't believe the entire story. Least not yet.

"I can see the doubt on your faces. I understand your reluctance to believe. Why would I trust strangers over the people who'd raised me five long years? Easy. My father and his father wanted nothing to do with me. They just wanted to harness the power they thought I held. Nothing more. I went through day after day of training. No hugs or kisses like my mother gave me. No birthdays or friends. I trained and I hated them. They were the reason my mother was snatched from me. Even still, I didn't blindly take Squire's word as truth. He gave me a cardboard box that contained items from my mother."

Damien watched as the doubt ran from Beth's face when Lily's voice cracked.

"Among numerous personal items was a letter urging me to trust Squire and anyone he instructed me to. It was in her handwriting and as I held my mother's note, the image of her tearfully writing it came clear. I've been loyal to Squire ever since."

He believed her. But sadly nothing she said brought him any closer to finding Grace.

"Some in the society are only members for the prosperity. Their hearts aren't committed to the extent of the elders'. They are the true dark-hearted ones. It's not just the money. They thrive off the power that rides hand in hand with dark magic. Feed off misery and pain, and therefore do all they can to cause it. True evil in the form of men. And women I should add. Women seem drawn to the danger. I can't count how many vied for membership and aren't here now from failing in one task or another."

"What do you mean fail?" he and Beth asked at the same time.

"The elders give out challenges. Those who pass are deemed worthy of lifetime membership. As you can imagine, there are no do-overs or temporary statuses. You are either in and pass, or you die." Lily's expression grew grim and he had no doubts the poor girl had seen more than her share of wickedness and death in her short time with the Society.

"The tasks were quite gruesome. The worst were often doled out to those members they understood couldn't complete them for sheer entertainment purposes. The idiots never saw their demise coming. So greedy for what they didn't have, they'd rather die than not try."

In his time with Octavia, he'd seen men battle for her attentions. Human men she hadn't cursed, only killed. The morons thought they warred for beautiful arm-candy. A trophy wife to display and brag about in front of their friends. He hated Octavia and hadn't given a damn about her. She was evil. But watching the humans and what they'd tried to pull over on her made him question where mankind had gone as whole.

"Do you remember the kidnapping of the high-ranking congressman who came to town on a visit? He was found dead, as well as his alleged kidnappers."

"Yeah, the story made headlines. Happened a few towns over." Beth replied. Damien watched Beth wobble a bit. He worried about her, but within a second Moss was at her side. Offering his strength.

Grace, to his knowledge, had no one right now. Wherever she was, whomever she fought, she did so alone and the fact ate at Damien's soul. Everything within him shouted to go, move, fight…do something. He hated he had no choice but to listen patiently in the hope something shed light on Grace's whereabouts.

"Yeah. A woman named Samantha was given the test to lure the married congressman to her bungalow. They instructed her to seduce him, and they, the society, would be taking photographic evidence. She was ordered to kill him after their tryst and return to headquarters, which by the way, moves every so often."

"I gather things didn't go as planned?" Damien shot Moss a look. This Society far more dangerous and larger than either originally suspected.

"No. I became aware of her fate when I came across the elders watching the video surveillance of the event."

"You don't have to go over this again." Squire placed a hand on her shoulder, but Lily shook her head, intent on explaining just how evil this group was.

"I agree with Squire. You owe us no further explanation." Moss gentled.

"Oh don't I? I'm not convinced you truly understand the level of dark they are. Octavia, my grandmother, was a saint compared to the rest of them."

"Finish your story," Beth urged, surprising them all.

"Other members had been given the test to kill *both* of them. They were aware Samantha was a member of the group vying for entry, same as them, and it hadn't mattered. The things they did to both…to her before they slaughtered them and," Lily's hand covered her mouth and her eyes closed as if she feared vomiting, "ate part of their remains."

"Oh my fucking God. Did you say ate?" Beth visually turned green, Moss hung his head and Damien just felt even more crazed to find Grace.

"They took turns pleasuring themselves with both, then stabbed, strangled, and slowly killed them. When they were dead, one ate her heart and the other member ate the congressman's. Not only were these sick bastards laughing while viewing the tape, but they were dining during the show."

"The news only reported the deaths seemed ritualistic. I understand now what gave them the impression," Beth whispered, still rather queasy in appearance.

"After the horror of what I'd witnessed, I began investigating. I mean I'd understood the group was bad, but not straight out crazy people-eating evil. I'd been told my mother chose to leave rather than stay. Had prayed she'd been forced to leave, but still lived and fought to find a way back to me. But I think on some deep level I knew she would never have left me. In my snooping I discovered they'd killed her. In the same bungalow as the murdered pair I watched on the video."

"Wait. Crap, I can't believe I forgot about this." Beth bounced off the counter she'd been leaning against like her ass caught fire.

Chapter Nineteen

Though now little more than a pile of dry rot toothpicks, Grace curled up under the faint cover of the cabin she and Henry had started together before he'd vanished. Old memories wove in comforting fashion around her heart and were the only things blocking the ivy vines of darkness trying to root within.

Bits and pieces of Demetrius still clung to the remnants of her dress and though a warm breeze carried over the placid waters before her, she shivered uncontrollably.

She'd killed them. Killed Damien.

Grace sunk to the ground beneath her, which after all the years of abandon was now more dirt than floor, and hugged her knees to her chest. Sobbing, she rocked back and forth grieving all the things that should have been and would be no more.

Her life with Henry. The happiness they'd vowed to create for themselves. She even remembered the first piece of wood they hammered up when building commenced on the shack she now sought shelter within. If she knew then she would end up here, within the paradise they thought they'd built, broken and alone …

No, I wouldn't give up one damn moment of my time with him. There were happy moments here with Henry.

Though construction stood unfinished, one night he'd set up a surprise. He'd blindfolded her and drove her out here. Carried her over the threshold of what was to have been their honeymoon suite and home. God, she could swear she still smelled the salmon he'd smoked. Henry made them their first candlelit dinner in their almost new home. She'd laughed because he'd been so proud of himself and then tripped over a two-by-four and dropped the bottle of wine. Grace peered over to a corner where her heart skipped a beat as she eyed the still stained wood.

She'd been so sure fate took mercy on her when Damien arrived in her life. She'd truly never thought to love again. How could any woman not take special note of him? Large, muscled and complete perfection. His dark hair, thick and long. His blue eyes so light they hypnotically drew you in. Hell, even his scent, smile and the way he laughed, rare as it may have been, promised untold pleasures. And even when she wasn't one hundred percent certain he returned her interest, least not in the long-term sense, she'd decided she'd go after him. Make him change his mind. That's how much the man affected her.

She found not a damn thing about him she didn't like. Well, except for his Bohemian attitude about her being the little lady. She'd been on her own far too long to cruise into such mentality. But given time he would have learned she was quite competent all on her own.

Or so she'd thought. Today proved otherwise and their lives were lost in her attempt at doing so.

Why didn't I wait? Damien would still be alive. Instead he lay dead, and all because of her recklessness.

No longer caring about a damn thing, she laid her head on the ground and watched the sunset in the lone window that remained in the tattered remains of her memories. She shut her eyes as the sun slid into her beloved swamp and prayed she never woke up.

• • •

He wasn't sure how, but Damien sensed Grace's distress. "What do you remember?" he asked to prompt Beth with her memory. "She mentioned years ago a place she and her fiancé built. Before he up and disappeared and all."

"Did she happen to mention where the place was located?" Now things were moving in the direction he needed. A direction which may lead him straight to Grace. He stalked toward Beth unintentionally aggressive, prompting Moss to step in front of her with a stance threatening retribution if he didn't cool his jets. He nodded to show his shit was in check. Barely, but nonetheless he would never harm Beth. But hearing a lead where Grace may be damn near felt like someone hooked up electricity to him. He was super charged and ready to bring Grace home where she belonged.

Home?

Fuck yeah. Grace was home. His dumb, hardheaded ass recognized the fact now. Gods be, he prayed his acknowledgement was not too late in coming.

"She never gave me an address. I just know it's a special piece of land hidden nearly in the swamp itself. She always glowed when she spoke of the place."

"She did?" Squire broke in.

Damien didn't like Squire's interruption nor the half-assed triumphant look on the man's face.

"Her heart shattered the day Henry never returned. But she never gave up hoping. Prayed one day he might come strolling in," Beth said.

"So she never went on to marry?" Again, the asshat Squire took them off course and continued to piss the fuck out of him.

"Can we get back on fucking track?" Damien tried to step between the hijacked conversation.

"She pined for years over the man. Hell, all the way up until she met…" Damien caught Beth's gaze flick his way before she trailed off. Grace's feelings toward him were a private matter. One which he intended on getting to the bottom of once he found her. He'd prove how much he loved her and would be a worthy mate.

"Then to find out he stopped fighting for her and decided to become one with the swamp creature he'd been cursed to share a soul with? Hell no. Aunt Grace is worth fighting for 'til the day she dies. So, he lost my vote."

"How are you aware of his fate? Are so sure of what transpired of her missing fiancé?"

"Well Moss and Damien heard rumor the some dipshit chose to turn into his animal counterpart. Yes, it may be only rumor and maybe it wasn't even him, but I doubt that considering the name overheard was Henry. The name of her missing finance. Rumor also had it that the animal was killed." Beth glanced at him then turned to Moss for confirmation. He nodded before attempting to get them back on track.

"Excuse me while everything Beth said is true—are we going to rescue Grace or continue discussing some deadbeat fiancé? Because if I have to head out and check every damn piece of shit shack on the swamp I will, but isn't it best for Grace if we try to jog your memory of where and speed up finding her?" Beth's attention swung back to him. She looked a little confused by the drilling Squire just put her through. Damien suspected the why, but shoved the thought to the back burner for now.

"I can't think of anything more details."

"Maybe a bend in the water or old oak trees…something?" he prompted Beth.

"I might have an idea where she is," Lily quietly spoke.

"How would you possibly know?" Damien saw the glint in Beth's eyes turn downright dangerous looking.

"Lily has visions occasionally," Squire offered quickly, but Damien smelled bullshit. The man was lying out his ass. But why? Even Beth picked up on the swift cover-up attempt as did Moss, judging by the slight nod he gave.

"So where then?" Her hands were planted on her hips, but the set in her jaw told Damien Beth was about to go off in a big way if Lily didn't answer fast and truthful. No more crap.

"It's at the end of what is now known as Heaven's End. I can lead you there, but I really wanted to stay close to the phones for word on Trick."

"Lily, come with me and we can check on Trick before leaving." Squire escorted Lily from the room before any of them could argue.

Once the three of them were alone, Damien came straight out with it.

"He's hiding something. Big."

"Damn straight he is. The lie's stinking up the whole room," Moss agreed.

"What are they all hiding from us and why? I thought the whole point in the invitation was to join forces in fighting the Society. Now, I'm wondering if this whole ruse was simply to keep us under their watchful thumbs." Beth slammed her palm down on the counter behind her.

"What do you mean?" Moss asked.

"While we've been here, they've been able to keep watch over our every movement." Damien answered for her, seeing where her line of reasoning headed.

"Exactly."

"I apologize for the delay." They turned to see Squire stroll into the room alone.

"Where's Lily? We need to leave. Enough stalling. Grace's life is at stake and now is no time for coddling the girl." Damien stated.

"I assure you, I coddled no one. Lily and Trick formed a rather special bond. One that has left her uniquely tied to him. It is in her best interest to return to the hospital and be by his side."

"I thought you said it was too risky for her to do that?" Damien questioned the sudden change in plans. What had changed since earlier when the girl begged to stay and now? All the unanswered questions simply snowballed and added to his sense of unease.

"Trick slipped into a coma. The doctors are stumped as to why his condition continues to worsen. They'd feared he wouldn't make it, then he rallied for the better. Out of the blue they claim his vitals became unstable again and has now drifted into the coma. I felt it best someone he's familiar with be at his side." Squire said.

Damien nodded in agreement. As much as he'd like to check on the kid himself, Grace's safety took priority. Always would.

"Lily gave me directions, which I wrote down. Are we ready to leave?" Squire abruptly changed the subject again, but Damien didn't give a rat's ass. He'd been ready and wouldn't be able to hold back his animal counterpart straining for its mate any longer. He stormed out of the room ahead of the others, and barreled for the front door.

"Guess that answers my question," he heard Squire mutter behind him.

He rode with Squire, this time in a Range Rover that Slick, Punge, and Branch had thoroughly checked for any booby traps, namely bombs. Squire even gave the vehicle a once over himself, as did Damien before climbing in. Didn't stop the nervous twitch Squire gave right before he turned the keys. Truth be told, Damien heard the hitch in everyone's breath when Squire turned the ignition over.

The ride for the most was short and quiet. Was Grace someone's captive or had she run to the symbol of her first love? And if so, what did this say about where her heart really lay?

He wasn't stupid. All he could offer may not be enough. Deep down Damien understood he'd never be able to offer her the kind of life Henry would have. The type she deserved…but damned if he didn't want her anyway. Wanted to try to make her every moment in life safe, happy and loved.

But very soon he might get the truth. Funny thing was, he wasn't sure he could handle it.

Chapter Twenty

They'd gone down more back roads than most would have been able to remember, but Damien mentally bookmarked each one of them. He'd never be somewhere and not find his way out. That said, he knew the swamps like the back of his hand. He'd always find his way home. Always.

Finally the Range Rover drew to a stop in front of a rickety half-built shack. Even as dilapidated as the thing had become, Damien envisioned the beauty of what would have been had things not gone awry for Grace and her beau. Sadness rooted deep for her. For the pain she'd endured alone.

"Can you feel the emotion radiating around us?" he heard Beth whisper to Moss.

"Yes. Like sorrow has woven around all life within this area." The slight rustling sound of a body moving indicated Moss had embraced Beth.

Smart man. Recognizes what he has and holds on tight.

Though sad for Grace, had her fiancé not disappeared, he and Grace would have never met, Damien mentally admitted. For this reason, and though he wouldn't have wished the evil of Octavia on any man, he would not lie and say a part of him wasn't glad the fiancé had vanished.

Grace belonged with him. Period. Now that his dumb hard-headed self had figured out his ass from his heart, anyone trying to get in his way would wish to their God they hadn't.

"She's here. I detect her scent," Squire said and his tone sounded…off. Damien wasn't sure what undertone he picked up from the man, but it had him ready to kill. Fighting back his territorial instinct to destroy Squire over the comment, Damien exited the car before Squire managed to get a leg out.

Damien cupped his hands around his mouth as he yelled, "Grace" and prayed for a response.

Silence.

"Grace. Are you here?" he called again as he moved toward the ruins, cautious and wary for any potential traps.

Silence.

"Oh God, what if she isn't?" Beth's voice broke as the question trembled from her lips.

Damien spotted the rickety dock that led out to the floating shack. The place sat situated half on land, half off, as a small waterway stood between land and home. He tested each plank and though the old weathered wood creaked in protest, it appeared to be able to hold his weight.

"We need to cross slowly and one at a time," he warned the others.

Each board cracked a little, but held strong as he made his way across. Beth was two steps behind him and Moss two behind her. Though the water was not drowning deep, its stagnate surface held numerous threats hidden beneath. Gators and snakes, two of the worst.

Once his foot finally made contact with what he assumed had once been a porch, he called yet again in desperation for Grace.

Silence.

The front area, barely standing, would not be able to withhold all of them. He motioned for the others to wait. Last thing he wanted to do was destroy the last remnants of a place Grace loved and cherished.

The three behind him decided to turn back, easing carefully off the equally disintegrating deck.

He fought the urge to race into the dilapidated dwelling and verify Grace hid somewhere within, but he feared any heavy footed movements would bring the place crumbling down.

"Grace. Sweetheart, are you here?" He lowered his voice, forcing the hard fear-laced edges down a notch.

The place had turned dark, but his nocturnal sight aided in seeing in every nook and hidden cranny. Finally, he made out a shape curled up a tight little ball.

Grace.

He went and knelt at the ground beside her. Pale, ice cold, and shivering in fierce abandon, he feared for her well being. How long had she been her like this? The air around wasn't nearly as cold as her body, and it looked like she was in shock.

"Grace, honey...talk to me," he soothed as he scooped her frail body in his arms. Her eyes remained clamped shut and he couldn't distinguish whether from real sleep, shock or refusing to acknowledge his presence. "Honey, you're scaring me. Come on, sweetheart. Wake up for me."

She seemed so small like this. Not the vibrant, headstrong woman he'd come to love and this fact scared the holy shit out of him right now.

"D...Damien? C...c...can't be. You're dead." Faint as her proclamation was, he caught her words.

"No honey. I'm fine. I'm right here." He stroked the sides of her face and shifted so she faced him. When she finally opened those gorgeous blue peepers of hers, he wanted her to see him. Proof he was very much alive. Hell, as her tantalizing scent reached his fear-addled subconscious, something else jumped alive as well. Normally he'd feel like a heel cradling her and getting wood, but if that was what it took to get her to believe he wasn't a dream, then so be it.

He lowered his mouth to her ear.

"I'm not the only presence alive right now, Grace. No way you can't tell—Junior says hi. Wake up for me now. Let me prove just how fine we are. Open those pretty blue eyes. Let me in, Grace." Relief flooded when her hand, shaky as it was, reached up to move a lock of hair from his eyes.

"I don't understand. You're dead. I heard the explosion. Demetrius said…"

"Whatever he told you were fabrications of the truth. No one died." Though Trick still fought for his life, Damien's words were still the truth.

"Promise me no one died. Promise me. Please, oh please, oh please." Her voice wavered and again, the sense she perched on the verge of shock caused panic to flare in him.

"No one died." He didn't count Demetrius as a someone, so he wasn't being computed into the equation.

"Beth?" Weak, but her voice strengthened the longer they spoke.

"Is just fine and outside this dwelling."

"Moss?"

"Moss is fine, too. They are outside with Squire. Waiting for us to come out." He wished he had a way to alert them, but he didn't dare leave her side yet. He wanted her talking and alert. The more she did, the better she looked. Her color even appeared to be returning.

"I thought I'd killed you." A keening wail burst from her, and she began rocking again. He couldn't let her slip back to where she'd been. Gripping her waist, he sat her up on his knee. With one arm crooked behind her, he used his free hand to force her gaze back to his.

"You didn't, so don't leave me again. Stay with me, Grace. I've been too stubborn to acknowledge all the emotions hitting me, but damn it, I love you. Ever since that day on your porch when you trusted me enough to open up. Since I massaged your shoulders and your scent, tears and laugh drew me in like a bat to a cave."

Silence.

"Did you," sniff, sniff, "just reference me like a bat to a...a... cave?"

Okay, in hindsight his rendition of their magic moment may not be the most romantic of descriptions. But he lived in a cave. Bats loved caves.

"Um. I'm not the best at..."

Damien found himself pleasantly cut off by a warm set of plump lips. She may have meant for the gesture to be sweet. But it was so damn much more. The satin lips sliding across his stirred the hunger within. His tongue swiped between their softness, urging them to part. Let him in. His animal surged forth happy its mate was back. His hand ran the length of her back, wanting more than to be stroking fabric. He needed to touch her. Skin on skin. Proof she was safe and within his embrace, where she belonged.

Her moan elicited a direct call to action from him. His tongue ran the length of hers, swirling 'round and 'round as they dueled in the most basic of all dances. He brought her body flush against his, languishing in the soft curves of his woman against him... safe. Felt the press of tight puckered nipples poke against his chest and wished others weren't waiting. He'd take her right here and now on this weathered old floor and implant himself within the memories of her past. Give her new ones to cling to while burying the old.

Grace kneeled then rose enough to lift a leg over his waist until she sat on his hard cock. Her hips rocked back and forth as she ran her crotch over his bulge. Her small puffs, pants, and tilting pelvis told him her gyrating hit all the right spots. Sure, he could have lifted her dress and been in her in a matter of one blink. He needed her as much it appeared she needed him. But Grace was too classy a woman for him to chance them being caught.

If he didn't call out to the others soon, they'd be barging in.

Pulling his mouth away he rested his forehead against hers, their hair blending to create the perfect of private canopies around them.

"No…don't stop. Please, I need you. Need more. Was so cold and now am…"

"Am what? Alive? Sultry? Yes, you are. Smoking hot. But sadly we aren't alone."

"What?" That grabbed her attention and had her smoothing her dress back down while glancing behind them in a nervous fashion. "Oh my God, I forgot what you'd said about others." Her face blushed the most beautiful shade of crimson he'd ever seen. Far more lovely than even the exotic bloodwood blooms that sprang up around the swamps in springtime.

"Uh, Damien." Her expression had become most quizzical. Almost humorous as she pointed behind them.

He turned to see four young armadillos standing there watching them.

"They're staring," Grace quipped as a smile spread across her face. "Your doing, I gather?"

"Not that I'm aware." He patted his thigh and the four armored creatures waddled right over.

"They didn't even hesitate." Grace seemed awed at the link he had with his cousins of sorts. Amused, he watched as Grace reached and gently picked one up. The thing curled into a ball, but once she brought it gently up into her arms, uncurled in tentative trust. Apparently even his little friends recognized Grace for what she was. His mate.

The moment was perfect as all became one. One with the swamp and the world that encircled its grace and beauty. Out here in the swamp as dangerous as it could be, life was simple. There were no outside confusions. The circle of life was that which it had always been. Survive. If you found a mate in the process… even better.

But as Damien glanced to the open door jamb, he knew things wouldn't be simple for them. Trick fought for his life, Squire hid something and after all the traumas, they needed to decide whether to remain with B.E.A.R. or not.

His vote was to take Grace back to his cave where he could protect her far better. Convincing Grace of this, however, would be an up creek row without an oar.

"Hello, Grace." The armadillos scattered, scampering back through the gaping holes in the ragged walls.

Damien jerked his attention to the door. Squire. Asshat had to ruin the moment. Sure, the magic was bound to end within a few minutes anyway, but damn. Squire couldn't have given them one more second?

Chapter Twenty-One

Grace's body froze within his arms. Her skin chilled even more than it already was as her gaze slid toward Squire. She eased from his grasp and rose before turning to face the man who'd intruded on their moment.

"I…how?" she stuttered as her mouth dropped open only to close and reopen again. Under different circumstances he would have teased that she resembled a guppy. Or followed his ungentlemanly thoughts when seeing those lush full lips of hers open and close. Not now though. His gut roiled and instinct told him to tread carefully or lose her forever. Something big was happening, and the fact he didn't understand what made him all the warier.

"You're dead. They told me you merged with the swamp creature you'd been cursed with. So how are you here? Now?"

"Grace, I…" Squire, too, seemed at a loss for words. Damien had been content riding shotgun in the backseat of this ride until Squire took hesitant steps toward Grace and his hands reached out for her.

"Whoa there, buddy. I don't think so." He placed himself between them and bit back the growl his beast wanted to unleash.

"Damien, it's okay," Grace promised, placing a hand on his forearm, her voice barely above a whisper. She'd come from one shock and sounded as if she headed straight into another.

"Who is he to you?" Damien's gut screamed he didn't want to hear her answer, but his mind knew he needed to listen to the truth. And from her. Not the challenger before him.

"It's....Henry. My fiancé...er, ex-fiancé."

Red clouded his vision as rage boiled over within. This man had known about Grace and had stayed mum the entire time. Damien felt played. And nobody played him.

Nobody.

•••

Grace wished she'd had more time to think about Henry returning from the grave, but she didn't. The flesh beneath her palm hardened and she thought she heard a hiss even as she stared at Henry, whose pupils suddenly went oval as his eyes drew to slits. Damien, who stood before her one second, launched airborne the next in one swift move into Henry...whom he'd called Squire. The world splintered as the massive men flew into the dilapidated wall and the rotten wood disintegrated around them.

A loud splash and Grace ran to the old dock to try and find out where they'd landed.

"What the hell is going on now?" Beth hollered, stomping her foot from the other side of the dock. Then her niece caught sight of her running out onto the dock. "Grace!" Beth screamed her name before she beelined toward her. Beth had taken only a few steps when one of the boards gave way and she nearly sank in the water and muck. Moss grabbed her around the waist and hauled her to shore before anything more than her feet hit the water.

"I'm fine, stay there," Grace yelled across to Beth and Moss before searching the water frantically for the dueling men.

Both rose out and Grace realized they'd gone into their animal counterparts. Or as much as she supposed either did. Squire's eyes looked lethal in appearance but held no candle to the predatory viciousness that damn near glowed from Damien's. His lips drew back and the snarl turned into a loud roar. She'd never experienced such helplessness as she did then.

"No! Please stop!" she begged, though neither even so much as flinched. Water splashed and swirled around as the two men lunged, bashed and punched one another in the territorial battle.

Damien's arm flew from the water and arced as he brought his fist down into Henry's jaw with a sickening thud. She watched in horror as Henry's hands rose from the murky waters to display talon-like nails. Frozen, she watched shocked to the core as those talons flew across Damien's now exposed chest. Screamed when a crimson stain spread slowly across the top of thick swamp water. Still neither man paused in their assault on the other. She was relieved to notice that where she'd thought gaping wounds would appear from the slices, only minimal scratches were visible. Memory skirted back to something Moss mentioned. Damien carried traits of his soul creature, the armadillo. He'd inherited armor it appeared.

More shouting, more curses.

What played before her seemed more a death match than any sort of standard fight.

Bones cracked, flesh slapped the water, and she feared what lurked beneath it waiting for a chance to strike the men battling above. Gators thrived in the area as did water moccasins.

Something large bobbed to the surface just behind the men and she squinted to make out whether a limb or a gator. Finally the rough, bumpy snout of gator distinguished itself. The thing was massive—at least seventeen feet—and she couldn't see the entire length. A monster among gators and heading straight for the men. Yeah, they might have animal strengths and qualities, but against the massive beast, they wouldn't stand a chance. Especially unaware of the approaching danger.

She yelled a warning as two more green bumps emerged on each side of them. Neither man noticing the arrival of more predators. The men rolled as though already in a gator's jaws, yet she knew they weren't. Not yet anyway.

Desperation made her turn to beg for Moss's help. She thanked the fates she didn't have to ask. The large man was already diving into the water. Glancing over to Beth, she saw the fear on her niece's face and guilt set in. Beth's fiancé endangered himself because of an event she set in motion.

If anything happens to Moss…

Both men had again disappeared beneath the stagnant water. Moss surfaced once or twice without coming up with either of them, and panic set in that they were too late. That in their need for bloodshed the gators had taken them. As if in slow motion, she became aware of Beth screaming for Moss as he came up empty handed again. Tears burned the backs of her eyelids as she leapt into the water, no longer able to stay out of the fight and not caring about any critters lurking nearby.

Popping to the surface, Grace gulped a deep breath before someone grabbed her by the scruff of her neck and hauled her out of the water. After being unceremoniously dumped on the ground at Beth's feet, Moss dove back into water.

He hadn't made it two strokes when both Damien and Henry breached the water's surface, both riding the backs of gators.

She may not be cursed with any animal soul, but she didn't need to be to feel the shock from the gators' as they jumped and swished their bodies madly back and forth in an attempt to dislodge the men riding them. Never before had she witnessed anything like the craziness before her.

"Get your ass back up here," Beth admonished to a weary looking Moss. Her niece flung herself into the giant's arms and held him tight before pulling him to the ground and sitting on him, swearing he'd better not think about heading back in the water.

Grace sat in the mud that surrounded her. Both men were safe and the overwhelming weight of the knowledge that mere days ago she'd had an idea which direction her life headed and now as she sat stinky and muck covered, she didn't know her ass from end.

Damien and Henry skulked in her direction, stopping just shy of where she sat. Confused and awkward in her own skin, her sudden uncertainty rendered her immobile. Both clearly sought something from her, but she didn't know how to answer. Hell, she didn't even understand the question. "Thank God everyone is okay." Beth started sounding clunky while trying to change the atmospheric gloom around them. Moss shushed her and gently pulled her away from them. Somehow her niece's he-man understood the unspoken mystery of her situation. Had put two and two together and figured out the panic attack s headed her way.

"Grace, we need to talk," Henry started.

"I'm not sure we do, Henry…er, Squire I should say. Correct? Your new name for your new life? Must be nice just to create a new one. Good for you." Yeah, maybe her voice did hold a bitter edge. But damn it. That's what came out. She'd pined for years over him. Worried he'd died in gruesome fashion. She'd been relieved over the rumors he'd been cursed and chosen to become his inner animal rather than some cross between. But that hadn't been what happened. He'd simply picked up and gone on without her. So that's exactly what she did now. Picked herself up, brushed her ass off and stormed over to where their vehicles should be parked.

"Grace, please let me explain…"

She whirled around. Gone was confusion. Now she was just angry.

"Explain what, Henry? How I wasn't enough for you? How fighting for me, for us, wasn't what, a worthy enough cause?" Hysterical? Yeah. She didn't care.

"She's been through enough for one day. Back the fuck off." Damien stepped in front of Squire and laid a firm hand on his chest. The thump echoed where hand met chest. She thought for sure Henry was about to attack when she caught the nasty look he shot Damien, but he must have thought better of it as he knocked Damien's hand off and stormed away.

The tears came then. She couldn't have stopped them had she wanted, so she turned and climbed into the back seat of the vehicle before her. Whose vehicle didn't matter.

"Are you alright?" Beth asked quietly, sliding in next to her.

"No." Truth.

"Everything will turn out okay. I promise. You've been through a lot. You need rest."

She nodded in agreement.

"Look, you're going to hate this, but we are much closer to B.E.A.R than your cabin. We're heading back there." When she went to protest, Beth held up a hand. "You can get a shower and some sleep and when you wake up, we can head back to your place."

As much as she didn't want to go anywhere near anyplace having to do with Henry, she was exhausted and filthy. A hot shower sounded like heaven.

"Okay. But tomorrow we go home."

"I promise. Scout's honor." Beth put her hand over her heart before embracing her in a heartfelt hug. "We were so worried." She saw her niece glance over in Damien's direction. He stood outside the vehicle speaking heatedly with Henry. Moss appeared to be attempting to play referee between the men. All at once they stopped and Henry jerked open the driver's door, snapped his belt and slammed his door closed. His lips were pursed as if fighting to keep from saying something. Moss came and scooted in next to her, and Damien slid into the front passenger seat. He, too, appeared to choke on words that wanted to tumble forth.

The ride back to B.E.A.R. was unbearably quiet.

Her own thoughts veered to Damien. Why hadn't the man said something to her? She'd jumped into the water willing to die to protect him and he'd not uttered a real word to her since returning to land. Had he had a change of heart about their relationship? Did something happen when her magic unleashed and the bomb went off? Maybe he'd remembered about the magic and decided she was too much trouble.

So many things swirled in her mind. But the sudden distance from Damien shattered her more than anything else in her life ever had. She felt it deep in her soul.

Chapter Twenty-Two

Damien hadn't wanted to, but after careful consideration of Moss's suggestion, agreed with Squire to give Grace some space. She'd been through being kidnapped, thinking she'd killed everyone and then the sudden shock of seeing her dead fucking fiancé return from said dead. Now wasn't the time to demand she chose who she wanted to be with.

It seemed he and Squire had reluctantly agreed to a stalemate of sorts. Even so, Damien parked a chair outside of Grace's room. Didn't trust the bastard's word he'd steer clear of her.

Damien kicked back on the chair legs and shut his eyes. These last hours were more than torturous. Not knowing if Grace was dead or alive. Much as he wanted to be angry at her cold shoulder, deep down he could admit he didn't entirely blame her. She had a lot of heavy emotional baggage going on all at once.

He understood her confusion. Prayed once she'd slept a good night's rest would come to her decision with a clear head and heart. Hoped beyond hope her choice led her to back to him. Her uncertainty ripped straight through his heart. Hell, his soul felt wounded like the bomb had exploded within.

What the hell can I offer other than my love?

Squire owned a freaking luxury compound filled to the brim with the most advanced security equipment and even designer furniture. The entire place was customized. By all appearances the man had the power to give Grace whatever her heart desired. Would be able to give her everything she deserved and more. Was he being a selfish bastard to linger and make her choose?

"Hey, buddy. How you holding up?" Moss stood before him holding out a bottle of water.

"Hanging in."

"You look like shit," Moss joked, but his voice held a hint of concern.

He'd grown close with the man as of late. The closest he'd found to a true friend in, well, far too long. "Thanks…ditto."

"Yeah, been a rather bitch week hasn't it?" Moss mumbled.

"Damn straight it has."

"Dude, relax. She loves you. Even I can see that…"

Before he finished his sentence, Beth strode out from across the hall, purse slung over her shoulder and appearing pretty weary herself.

"You ready?" she asked, passing by Moss to come over, lean down and hug him. "Everything will work out, you'll see. Trust your instincts, Damien." She gave him a peck on the cheek before turning back to Moss. "We really should get going to the hospital." Her voice grew grave as did the expression on her face.

"What's up? Has Trick's condition changed?" Damien felt like a heel. He should be down by the kid's side instead of sitting here like an overzealous boyfriend. He started to rise when Moss placed a staying hand on his shoulder.

"Yes. Unfortunately he took a turn for the worse. But he's in ICU and they are only letting one visitor in at a time considering he still hasn't regained consciousness."

"We're heading down more in support of Lily than anything else. Poor thing has refused to leave the hospital for any reason. Apparently if not for Trick covering her with his body, the shrapnel he took would be in Lily," Beth added, shaking her head lightly. "Kid was a true hero. And here I thought, well…"

"We'd all wondered about his loyalties, Beth. But we took him in anyway." Damien rubbed a hand through his hair. Damn but things continued to become ever more twisted and fucked up.

Poor kid had wanted nothing more than to fit in and he'd given him grief. If the kid pulled through, he'd find a way to make it up to him. Beth was right. Trick was a hero. Not only had he survived being kidnapped and God only knew what else by the Society, but now had taken a so-called bullet for Lily.

"Stay here. You can't help Trick right now. We'll keep you posted as we hear anything. Watch your girl and keep an eye out for Squire. I'm not sure I trust the guy." Moss warned before turning to follow Beth.

Damien nodded. He didn't believe a damn word Squire uttered either, but without proof and with Grace so fragile at the moment, he didn't want to cause any more drama.

Beth and Moss disappeared down the hall and questions raced through his mind. Curious why and how Squire could have stayed away from Grace all these years and why the man was lying. Dude definitely was. Damien just wasn't sure about what. This coupled with the extremes over the past few days versus little sleep, he drifted off.

Damien awoke to the sounds of voices. Loud and arguing. He sat the chair down on all fours as quietly as possible and glanced at his watch. He'd slept through the night. He prepared to barge in when the arguing stopped. He did something he'd never done before and wasn't proud of. Tried not to, but failed miserably. He listened outside the door not giving a damn what it might look like to any watching the halls from the security room.

"Yes, I loved you. I mourned for years over you. When you disappeared, a part of me died. A part that's never come back."

Damien's heart plummeted hearing Grace's heartfelt confession to Squire, especially when his advanced hearing caught the slight hitch in her voice.

"I never meant to hurt you. Quite the opposite, Grace. I steered clear for *you*."

"You abandoned me, for me. What the hell kind of sense does that make?"

"I wasn't the same man you were betrothed to. I was a freak of nature, no longer entirely human. I thought it best…"

"You thought it best. What about what I thought? What I wanted? Did you think so little of me as to truly think any changes in you would have made a rat's ass? That I would love you less because you'd been attacked and cursed by an evil bitch?"

Damien smirked when her voice rose to a near hysteric but highly pissed sounding level.

Give him hell, love.

"No, you twisted my words. I meant I dreamt of more for you. I wanted you to have an easy life. Without problems. A large house, white picket fence and two point five kids."

Same fears Damien had. He couldn't offer any of those things to Grace. Or at the very least, not right now. On this, he agreed with Squire. Grace did deserve those dreams. And many more.

He could be called many things, but self-centered was not one of them. Damien lowered his head and placed a palm on the door before easing away. The walk down the long hallway leading away from Grace was the longest walk he'd ever taken.

They'd loved each other once. Grace and Squire. They could find love again. Squire, or Henry as she called him, would be able to provide her a good, safe and loving home.

Knowing Grace was safe, happy, and well provided for would be enough.

It would have to be.

• • •

"I never asked for any of that. I only wanted you. Yet you took my choice away. I suffered over fear of what happened to you." She sighed and turned away, pulling herself in check. The last thing she wanted to do was fight with Henry. Shocked? Of course. Was she happy he hadn't perished all those years ago? Hell yes she was. He was alive and she could brush his ass off just the way she planned to now. "We've become different people. And no, I'm not talking about whatever creature you share your soul with." Part of her was curious and wanted to know what creature. But if she was ending things with him officially, asking would be too personal a question.

"Go ahead, ask me anything, Grace. We used to share everything. Our dreams, lives, bed and bodies." His voice went all smoky-like as he maneuvered toward her.

She shivered as memories came back. Of the happy times they'd shared. He must have seen the question in her eyes and though there was a small part of her that wondered what giving into Henry would be like, her heart had other notions. It wondered where Damien was.

Henry continued coming closer and he had the familiar look that at one time in her life, she swooned over. But even though his voice sent ripples coursing through her, they were nothing like the ones Damien prompted.

She placed her hand on his chest stopping him from getting any closer.

"While you will always hold a near and dear place in my heart as my one first love, I love another."

"Damien."

Stated, not questioned and Grace wondered what happened during her absence. "Yes."

"He makes you happy?"

"I think he could, yes." She hadn't known how else to answer except with the truth. Still unclear how Damien felt about her though her heart told her to follow him, and follow she would. She'd been gifted with a second chance at love, and she'd be damned if she let anything or anyone spoil that chance.

"Think?" Hope flickered in Henry's eyes.

"We haven't caught a break since our getting *sort of* together. It's been one damn thing after another." She huffed, and tossed her hands up in the air, disgruntled over all the bullshit they'd gone through.

"Then let me give you a gift and the promise that if you ever—and I mean ever, need me, I'll always be here for you, Grace. Promise me, you will always remember that."

She wondered what he meant by gift, but his words touched her heart and soul, as well as lifted the heavy stone of uncertainty and guilt that weighted her shoulders.

"I promise."

Henry leaned over and she worried for a minute what his intentions were. But he gave her a platonic soothing hug and as they broke apart pulled up one of her hands. He opened her palm and placed a set of keys in the center.

"What are these?" The keys jangled, and she tossed them lightly up and down in her palm, testing their weight.

"They're to a small cottage I own down on Sanibel Island. A small cove, less traveled, and no one, until you, even knows about. It was a place of escape and reflection for me. Go get Damien and go somewhere private. Spend some time with him, and make sure he's the one."

She saw the truth in his words. No tricks. Just peace for her and Damien to discover themselves and their relationship.

"What are all the other keys to?" Far more than a cottage key jingled about the large round ring.

"The one marked Ford is to the black Explorer sitting in the garage which is yours to borrow. The small one is to the entrance gate at the cottage. I meant what I said, Grace. I will always be here for you."

Henry stepped back, giving her a clear path to the door and Damien. She opened it, ready to tell Damien about Henry's offer of a small vacay to his cottage, but discovered an empty chair and vacant hallway.

Walking the few steps to Beth and Moss's room, she rapped a few times and waited anxiously. Honestly, she couldn't remember the last time she'd felt this excited about anything. When no one answered, she turned in confusion to Henry.

"Maybe they headed to the hospital to check on Trick."

"Trick? Why? What happened?" Her stomach roiled and her heart dropped. Her gut was right. After Henry explained about Trick fighting for his life and why…well, she understood Damien's absence. He'd grown close with the kid, as much as he tried to deny it.

Did he blame her for Tricks injury? If she hadn't made that foolish move with Demetrius odds are the bomb wouldn't have gone off.

Oh who was she kidding? Demetrius was stark raving mad. The loon would have set off the bomb whether she'd attacked him or not. She knew this. Wouldn't second guess herself.

If anyone should be pissed off, it was her. She liked Trick too. Had every right to be by the kids side too. In fact, Damien had lied to her. Told her no one had died. So, Trick hadn't died then… but fuck all, things didn't sound too good. And what did Damien do?

Vanished.

Again.

Even if only to the hospital. He should have at least offered to take her with him. She had to find him. Set things straight about Henry if nothing else. If he wanted to jet when she was done, so be it. But damn it, she would at least get the courtesy of a goodbye from him this time.

Chapter Twenty-Three

It took all of two minutes to call Beth as she grabbed her purse to discover Damien hadn't left for the hospital with them. Beth briefed her in polite fashion about Damien's mindset about Henry. Panic set in and Grace raced down the corridors, desperate to find him. They'd been through too much not to get a chance to explain about Henry.

Damn the hardheaded ass. But she loved him.

Grace refused to let another male make a decision concerning what she wanted or deemed acceptable in her life. Grace began backing from B.E.A.R's garage when a figure jumped behind the vehicle.

Fuck! She slammed on the brakes and prayed the idiot managed to maneuver clear of her path quick enough.

Her door ripped open and strong arms snaked around her, yanking her slap out of the vehicle.

"Grace, I don't own shit. But before you decide to give that moron Squire, or Henry or whoever the hell he, is a second chance, know that no one will ever love you as much as I do. Love is all I have to offer at the moment, but I will do everything within my power to take care of you. To see that you never want or lack for anything. Give me a chance to prove myself."

Before she could assure him she'd been on her way to find him, Damien's arms locked around her, caging her against him. Hot lips crashed over hers and delicious flutters ran amok through her. Her body warmed and southern area grew moist as her mind became mush. All that mattered was …

Damien.

Being with him. Them together. Nothing else.

Her back hit the cool metal of the Explorer and her feet lifted from the ground. Instinct and gravity forced her to wrap her legs around his waist. His tongue delved deep and mingled with hers. Challenging hers to play. Her breasts became achy and she knew her nipples poked through the thin tee she wore. His hiss when he broke away from her mouth assured her Damien was quite aware of her aroused state. Warm lips trailed her jaw and neck as he pumped against her.

Ah, so she wasn't the only one turned on right now.

The rock hard bulge in his pants hit her in just the right spot. Her thighs trembled around his waist as she rocked against his thrusts, getting more and angry at the amount of clothes that stood between her and ecstasy. Talk about a body zinging to life. Yowza.

"Need you."

His voice was rough and timbered and striking chords in her all on its own. He lifted her hair off her neck and began suckling one specific spot. She nearly giggled over the notion she'd be sporting hickeys tomorrow. But the strong pulls and the stronger thrusts sent her head reeling and her nether regions squirming. Her tee slowly rose as Damien drew it higher and higher until it bunched under her chin, and the mouth which had been diligently working her neck moved lower, latching onto a nipple through her sheer bra. Blunt teeth bit the engorged bud and had her squirming against him even more.

"Damien. Oh shit…yes," she cried as his teeth gripped the edges of her bra. Yes, off, now.

"Geez, get a room already."

She never thought she'd moved so fast in her life. Her feet flew to the ground. Her nose slammed into Damien's back when he whirled around to block her near naked state.

"Whoa, dude. I coughed when I came out. You two didn't so much as flinch. We're heading down to the hospital. Things aren't looking good for your friend." Branch held his hands up in the air.

She popped from behind the wall called Damien.

"What's happened?" she squeaked, both embarrassed yet worried sick.

"Lily called. She was bawling. Between her gasps she said Trick's vitals were becoming unstable, then a weird beeping started and she hung up."

"Were you able to talk with anyone else?" Damien paled as he asked and she knew he felt responsible for the kid.

"No. I heard your friends, Beth and Moss, in the background trying to offer comfort, and right before the phone disconnected..." He looked off appearing to dread what he said next.

"What did you hear?" Grace came around Damien and lined herself up to jump in the driver's seat of the Explorer.

"Your friend Beth cried out, 'Oh God no.'"

Branch hadn't finished before both she and Damien were in the Ford backing out. Grace hit the gas and they sped off for the hospital.

"Damien, I'm so sorry. Oh God, you should have told me what happened. You shouldn't have lied. My actions prompted..."

"No, it wasn't your fault. I didn't tell you because of the fragile state you were in. I feared the truth of his condition would have set you further in shock. It wasn't a lie to hinder, but to help."

Tears flowed freely as she drove and her gut told her Trick was gone. The poor kid hadn't stood a chance against the evil they were up against. Damien's hand came to rest on her knee. A light squeeze drew her attention to him. His eyes were wet, though no tears fell.

"No matter what we find, we will get through it together." His voice was solemn, but she knew without a doubt they would. They would eventually go to their borrowed ocean retreat and rekindle the fires that burned deep. Bond closer than ever before and cement their fledgling relationship.

But for now their strength was needed elsewhere. And they would offer it together, standing firm by each other's side and though they headed to heartbreak, they would weather it, united as one.

Just as they had all the other storms. Together, true and strong under the gentle rays of their beloved swamp's full moon.

More from This Author
(From *Swamp Magic*)

The swamp air sat heavy on her skin, as her water-soaked feet sank deep within the bog's smelly muck. With each mud-laden step, Beth was certain she would lose one, if not both, of the fugly combat boots her brother had insisted she wear. She'd cursed him at the time, but was now more than grateful to have on the snake-proof boots. Whenever she found Robby's ass and they got out of this godforsaken place, she'd kill him. No, scratch that. Skin him, then kill him.

Damn, but she should have listened to Kara and kept her butt at home rather than gone out traipsing through this mosquito-infested, hot as Hades swamp, trying to track down some elusive-ass bog monster. She'd ignored her best friend, listening instead to her whacked-out brother while her inner Nancy Drew leapt at the prospect of a mystery. Now she was wandering lost, in the swamp…at sunset, no less. She'd rather be at home getting ready for bed, and hopefully another night with her dream man. Her faceless hero, whom though she'd never seen, knew would play some important part in her life.

But no, color me stupid. She'd let her brother talk her into it. She was hot and miserable as she slapped at yet another mosquito while silently cursing herself.

Irritable, she plucked at her sweat-soaked tee. She didn't think she'd ever been so stanky in her whole life. A quick sniff to her pits served as confirmation. Good grief, surely the bog monster would hightail it in the opposite direction at the first ungodly whiff of her. So would any other living thing, she prayed, since darkness had fallen, and the night creatures had come out to play.

An owl hooted right when she began to step over a log and right as something tapped her thigh. Her scream hit octaves she hadn't known she possessed as some fast-paced high kicking had her precariously perched atop the next closest log.

Shaking, it took her a few minutes of squinting through the darkness with only the aid of her fading flashlight before she realized her attacker was just a limb floating by. Whew. She'd feared a gator, or, worse, a slithery snake or lizard.

Beth glanced about, if not for being lost, she'd almost be relieved no one was around to see her right now. Right, like who the hell would see? She was in the middle of freaking nowhere and worried about someone seeing her acting like a big weenie and not the capable self-sufficient woman she was.

Shaking her head, she sat and tried to gather her bearings. Reaching behind her, she grabbed a wad of humid frizzy hair and attempted to plait the jet-black mess enough she'd be able to tuck the end inside the plait itself. The loose tendrils stuck to her back and face, driving her batshit crazy.

Okay, now think, Beth, think. You last saw Robby and his doofus buddies by the old shack. You then, like a dumb-ass, went searching for them heading east...so said shack should be around the bend, a little more west.

Certain of her whereabouts, she cautiously stepped off the log, noting the thick, lily-pad-covered water swirling to her right and said a quick prayer that whatever caused the swirl wasn't deadly. The last snake she'd seen had her climbing a cypress tree faster than most of the raccoons she'd passed.

Maybe if she moved really fast? No, predators were attracted by quick movements. Fast might not be the best idea. Almost hypnotically, her gaze drew back to the swirling, as the water almost seemed to turn iridescent. She shone her flashlight more toward the center, whacking the dying metal thing on her palm a few times to no avail. Relief washed over her when she saw no evidence of red glowing eyes lurking nearby. The glow, a sure telltale sign of gators lying in wait.

Shit, why the hell hadn't she paid more attention to those damn survival shows her brother always made her endure? What was the one show, *Man Against Wild?* Well, how about *City Brat Against Wild?* Wild would win, without a doubt.

She scanned the area again and prayed she had indeed headed in the right direction. If not, she faced a long, tedious, and frightening night.

Well, she sure as hell wasn't getting to the cabin perched up on the damn stump. She wanted out of this godforsaken swamp with the humidity from hell. Not to mention getting away from the prehistoric-sized bugs swarming all around.

The water eerily stilled as the swamp sounds came to an abrupt halt. No screeching hoot owls, no more insanely loud chirps from crickets. *Nothing.* No movement or sound pierced the night. Complete and utter silence greeted her. The loss of the natural sounds terrified her more than anything else. Something had spooked the critters and bugs, and her gut screamed that whatever it was, with her luck, was so *not* a good something.

Time to go. She slid off the log and began wading toward the cabin—or, rather, she *hoped* toward the cabin.

She felt more than heard the water swirling about her calves and whipped around to search for its source. Her heart rate went into overdrive as her palms grew sweaty, making it harder and harder to retain her death grip on the flashlight.

Turning, she began taking cautious steps backwards toward the bend and the hopeful safety of the shanty she'd seen. Her beam was now so dim, the heavy-gauge metal was more weapon than light as she raised it over her head, aiming toward the swirls moving the deeper water to her right. In the midst of the strange whirlpools, the odd yet mesmerizing iridescence came back. Only this time it wasn't *almost* glowing—it *was* glowing. The eerie, greenish blue spiraled about madly, only visible here and there as it peeked out between the many lily pads, obscuring her view.

Terror gripped her, anchoring her in place as headlights do a deer over the freaky happenings before her. Trembling, her mind screamed to turn and run, but her body refused to heed her mind's clear warning. Her heart beat with such velocity she swore it would burst from her chest at any moment. She couldn't even seem to will breath into her body, and her lungs grew heavy. Her breathing became no more than ragged gasps as she began to hyperventilate.

Her eyes widened as the active water began to become more centered. Fear froze her immobile. Though terrified, she continued to be drawn, almost as if in a trance, into its strange murky depths. Her vision zeroed on the brightest point amid the swirls, jaw gaping open as a form began to emerge.

The form of a man.

He rose from the murky depths like some type of Greek deity, Neptune perhaps. Her mouth grew dry as he continued his slow rise, inch by glorious inch. Terror receded as blatant curiosity arose. She tried to lick her parched lips as droplets of water ran down his wet, chiseled chest and continued running until they disappeared into the low-slung waistband of his pants. Pants which, luckily for her, were good and wet and plastered to his magnificent body, leaving little to the rest of her imagination. She nibbled her bottom lip, wanting to lick just one of those lucky, lush little droplets rolling down him.

One jerk of his head moved the long, dirty-blond hair enough to reveal the face of a god. Eyes so intensely green she swore they penetrated her soul. And shoulders, oh, so big, they would devour her if she were embraced within. Bronzed skin that had been kissed by many a sunray, abs that rippled right down his belly. Part of a beautiful tattoo was visible as it spread about his stomach in a unique pattern, seeming to come from his back.

She'd gone mad. She should be running in stark fear, yet here she stood watching a man emerge from the swamp and wondering about being wrapped safely in those huge arms. Her fingers itched to run them over every hard, muscled ridge, all the way down to …

Too much heat—yes, that explained everything. She'd passed out from heat stroke and this was some weird delusion. *One smoking hot sex delusion at that.* It had been quite a while since she'd been with anyone intimately.

Her vivid delusion began heading straight toward her, a severe look drawn on his face, almost hungry and predatory in nature.

Holy smokes, she thought, licking her lips at the sight. Again her eyes drew toward what lay just below those fabulous abs as hip bones sculpted the most perfect V shape she'd ever seen. Her imaginary man would have been better completely and utterly naked; however, her luck seemed to have run out in that department.

The delusion seemed to beckon her as it stretched out a hand and one long finger pointed at her and began motioning her toward him. All the iridescent colors coming from him and the water began blending with the night and foggy air, swirling faster and faster in a tornadic display of light and color. Her head swam with it all, until from the heat, shock and fear, she succumbed to the pull of oblivion, and sank welcomingly into it.

Beth Sloan awoke slowly and very groggily to her head bobbing and the knowledge she was upside down. The water seemed much too far away now for her current liking. She threw out a hand to brace herself enough to sit up, and when it contacted warm, hard, living flesh, her eyes flew open at once.

In the mood for more Crimson Romance?
Check out *Loving Out of Time*
by Dorothy Callahan
at *CrimsonRomance.com*.

Made in the USA
San Bernardino, CA
10 May 2014